The Siren's Call

Jezebel Voulé

This edition published, 2023
001

Cover made on Canva
Illustrations made on Procreate by *Jezebel Voulé*

CuddlePuddleCo.com

ISBN: 978-1-961325-99-9

Dedicated to my support group.
I am often impressed by how many amazing
people have found their way into my life.
I'm thankful to you.

It was once commonly thought that the sea held no rules, generating fear in some and awe in others. From land, one may perceive the sea as a vast and bottomless pit. However, if humans knew the extent of the law that rules the oceans, the fear and respect given to the waters would surpass what any mere human can even fathom.

Forward: The story of Gaea

Once upon a time, there was only Gaea. Her body was yellow and barren, and loneliness swallowed her. As she listlessly wandered the cosmos, she searched for a connection, but there was nothing. So she wept. Her tears were dry and made of sand, causing deserts to spring from her sorrow. When she thought she would collapse from her melancholy, Uranos was born. He was a creature of air, and as he saw Gaea crying, he wrapped himself around her filling her with oxygen. Gaea loved Uranos not just because of the company he shared but because his love was instinctive and nourished her. As she joined in union with him, she bore many things. Her body became green and full of life with each child she created. She finally was filled with a purpose, to protect and house life. In her quest for creation, she was determined to make something grand. The progeny that had would forever alter her.

She bore the Cyclops first. They were big, strong, and many. However, with only one eye, they were limited in sight and found themselves slow and often clumsy. Even still, Gaea found love for them. Sadly Uranos did not feel the same. He had a distaste for such foolish and inept creatures, so he locked them away deep into the belly of Gaea. She bartered with Uranos, and he left a single Cyclops in solitude on the Island of the Cyclops as a homage to her first draft. Later to be referenced in the Adventures of Odysseus. She provided everything it would need and was gentle with the ill-sighted creature.

She created again, trying to improve upon the Cyclops, and made big strong creatures that she called giants. She had given them two eyes, and they were industrious and hard-working. Gaea was initially proud of her new, improved creations, but these large creatures often misstepped and injured her. Due to the destructive nature of the giants, all of them were locked away deep within Gaea's belly. As she cried out in pain, a new creature spawned. It was wet and fluid and filled her land with water. Uranos, being a protective partner once more, took the giants and locked them up with the Cyclops with the help of the creature born from her pain. Uranos called him Oceanus.

Uranos had taken a keen affection for Oceanus. They had bonded in the corralling of the giants, and seeing Uranos give respect to a creature filled Gaea with hope. She had worried that Uranos could not enjoy the company of the beings he inspired in her, so she flooded with ease as she saw their bond grow. She, too, was filled with inspiration for new creatures of Oceanus' design. Instead of many, she had decided that she would create a mere twelve in total, partly due to a fear that these progeny would join their brethren and get locked up within her depths. She yearned for her creatures to grow without being tucked away out of sight or mind. Six children held a masculine nature about them. They were called Titans and individually named Oceanus, Coeus, Crius, Hyperion, Lapetus, and Kronos. The other six she called Titanides collectively and were filled with feminine energy. Individually they were called Theia, Rhea, Themis, Mnemosyne, Phoebe, and Tethys.

Gaea often worried that Uranos' affection for these children would wane and they too would be locked up deep within her, so she asked her giants to take her ore and construct a scythe in secret. This scythe would protect her children from Uranos by cutting him down if needed. She refused to have any more of her children imprisoned by her partner. She, after all, was vibrant not only in strength but in will and was wild with enthusiasm green from having tasted a moment of fulfillment.

Uranos bowed to her upon the knowledge of the scythe. He knew she had breathed life into him and could remove it if desired. He was at her mercy, and so he became quiet. He broke his silence only on rare occasions, whistling a tune to put Gaea at ease because, despite their disagreement, his love for her was strong and true. In doing so, Gaea created many things, from blades of grass to human creatures.

The Titans and Titanides grew cocky, and eventually, the youngest of the Titans, Kronos, convinced his siblings to overthrow their parents and take over the world as it was. They locked Gaea and Uranos in the same pit as the giants and cyclops, destined to dwell there for all eternity.

Though Gaea had been imprisoned by her own creations, she was content to be able to be detained amongst her children. Uranos could not see that bright side. Everyone knew it was he who had slighted the children and was the direct reason for their imprisonment. Both Uranos and Gaea's children held disdain for the other. When Oceanus heard about their detention, he was devastated and broke into a million pieces creating streams, ponds, springs, and a myriad of different bodies of water, vowing never again to be whole until Gaea and Uranos found freedom.

Life is cyclic, and as Kronos and his kin had done to their mother and father, their children had done to them. It wasn't before long that the Titans and Titanides also found themselves imprisoned in the belly of Gaea. Kronos' son Zeus led a rebellion against the Titans, locking them away, fearing being overthrown for his crown. He destroyed the key that locked up the creatures of the past and vowed to destroy any that fathomed the idea of defeating him. He strategically put his brothers in charge of domains he had little interest. They diligently took guard of the land that Zeus had gifted them so that he could keep his rule, but nothing would rise from the sea nor the ethereal plane to challenge his crown. Zeus blessed his brother Poseidon to take to the waters, and Hades guarded the underworld as tokens of appreciation for their fidelity, and together they would rule all.

Chapter 1: The Woes of Atargatis

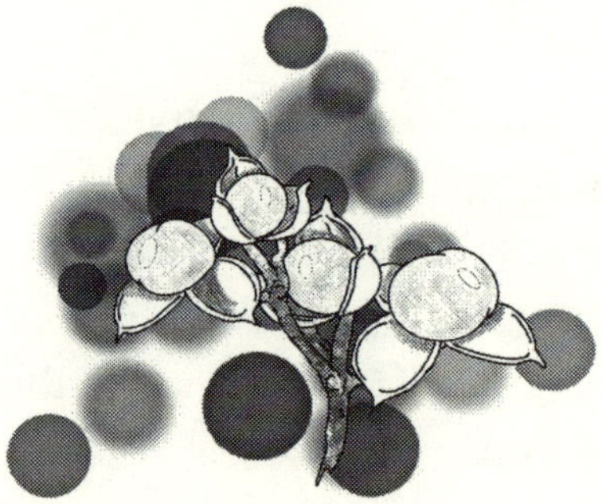

Then the gods ruled every day, man. As gods often do, they found humans to be toys to play with and feed upon. They were used to stave off their boredom and easily discarded once a god was satiated. Poseidon was best known for being the keeper of the seas and for his fondness for horses. He would often boast about how the character of a horse far exceeded man, and when he would visit the land, he would often transform into a stallion. Like many of the gods of his time, he would take offerings from women and did not worry about whether they were willing. It was a common practice at the time that harbor cities would send their prettiest maidens as a tribute to the god in exchange for good tides, calm seas, and plentiful bounty from his domain. If Poseidon chose to accept a maiden of sacrifice, he would pull them into the sea and do as he wished to the poor girl. When bored, he would abandon the girl in the depths, where they would eventually drown.

In the chance that the girl could swim, they were often too far out to make it to land, or another creature would take their turn brutalizing the woman until she died from exhaustion or a forced hand. This was the way of the world. Many accepted it with little to no question. It was as dangerous to be a woman that held beauty as it was to be a man of exceptional skill, as the gods often found jealousy when humans exceeded them in even the most mundane activities. At best, you would lose your life, and at worst, you would be cursed indefinitely. So it wasn't abnormal for Poseidon to visit various coasts and islands looking for his next play date.

It was in passing that Poseidon saw Atargatis. She was an Assyrian goddess who spent her time amongst her people, bestowing strength when they were fearful. The people would come to her as it was said that her kiss upon the belly could make the most barren of people ripe with child. She often was seen walking along the coast while bathing in moonlight. Her delicate features captivated all. When Poseidon saw her, he knew he would have to have her. So he approached her, and although she was polite, she refused his advances because her heart was already attached to a mortal named Adad. Her eyes sparkled, and her lip curled upward at the mention of his name. Poseidon tried to bribe her with treasures, and once more, she refused. A spurned lover, Poseidon left her that night, but he would not be slighted so easily.

The following day dressed as an average townsman, Poseidon tracked down Adad, a young shepherd who was kind and patient. He approached Adad and offered to buy all his wool so long as the sheep were sheared before him. Adad was thrilled to have such luck and welcomed the stranger's company. The townsman asked average questions that Adad had heard from many clients.

"How long had he been a shepherd?"

"How old were the sheep he was shearing?"

"How did he come to be a shepherd?" With each question, it wedged a little bit more personal. The townsman was curious about Adad as a person and less as a shepherd, which made Adad happy.

It was a natural conversation that led to the townsman asking about love. The second love was mentioned. Adad stopped shearing, looked up to make eye contact with the man, and beamed about a woman who held a flame to no one else. He spoke of her beauty, generosity, compassion, and the spark she inspired in him to want to be a better man. He loved her as he never knew love existed. As the townsman, Poseidon, listened, his disgust increased. She had not been generous with him. If she had been, he would have her body. She showed no compassion when she rejected his advances. She shared no sparks of love with him. With every word, his bitterness festered and grew. He would not stand to lose her affections to a mere mortal. To Poseidon, Adad was not just beneath a god like himself but also beneath his peers in the hierarchy of man.

It was time for him to intervene. He would have Atargatis. The statement 'No' was not an acceptable answer to the likes of him. She may have been a goddess, but she was beneath him and did not deserve the right to deny his advances. Despite this, he smiled. His smile grew as a plan unfolded until his beaming face matched Adad's. Poseidon leaned in until he was on the brink of being uncomfortably close to Adad's face.

"Can I give you something?" Poseidon loudly whispered. Intrigued, Adad stopped shearing and sat upright.

"What's that?" Adad asked. The townsman's smile grew even more comprehensive.

"I have a gift from the gods," the man replied as he pulled out a handful of berries. "These berries come from Aphrodite's garden. It is said that eating them and then kissing the person you love will bind your soul to your lover so that even in death, you can find each other in the underworld."

"Now, for mortals, it is a beacon to each other. No matter what, your soul will be bound to the other, and you will always know how to find each other. However, if you bind yourself to a god," he paused, and a wicked smile crossed his face, "Or in this case, a goddess," he continued, "You can call her, and she can appear before you. So no matter where you are in your journeys, you will never have to live a day without her. If you wish." Adad's eyes shone with intrigue.

"So I can call out to her, and she will be there, no matter how far inland I may go?" Poseidon slapped the backside of the ewe that stood between them.

"Exactly!" he said exuberantly. "It also can safely return her to the coast where she thrives best."

Adad couldn't tear his eyes away from the berries.

"Wha- What do you want in exchange for the berries?" Adad stammered.

"Let us just say I am a romantic and wish to give them to you as an early wedding gift." The townsman grabbed Adad's hand and poured the berries into it.

"You need to eat the berries an hour before you see her. Do not tell her about the berries. Once you've eaten them, kiss your beloved on the mouth, which will seal the bond. You will be connected forever. You must wait three days before you tell her of the bond. Upon telling her, she can choose to accept or not. If she accepts you can call her and she will appear. If she declines, you will know your love is untrue, and the bond will be broken." The townsman shrugged, feigning indifference to Atargatis declining the bond.

"I will warn you, though, if she knows anything about the berries from now until the three-day wait, the consequences will be dire. Aphrodite has no patience for love untrue."

Adad rolled the berries in his palm. They were soft and promised that they would be juicy. He smiled at the thought of always getting to see his beloved. Even if it was for but a moment every day. Could he have such luck? Then a thought crossed him, and his smile glimmered away.

"Why are you not using these berries?" he asked with a hint of distrust. The townsman smiled grimly.

"I have, alas, my wife met with the gates of the underworld during childbirth. I must remain here until my daughter has wed, and then I will once more return to my beloved," his eyes drifted into a place far beyond the stable's walls before snapping back to the young shepherd. "I want you to have the same joy as I do, knowing that though we are separated now, I will be with her again." Adad stood erect and grabbed the townsman, pulling him close in a firm embrace.

"Thank you," he whispered into the stranger's ear and then resumed finishing his shearing with haste as he wanted nothing more than to return to Atargatis' arms.

Poseidon had, in fact, obtained the berries from Aphrodite. They had been a gift from Hades to her and bloomed in her garden. He had been truthful that the berries could bond souls together for all eternity, and if desired, the two souls would find each other. Nothing could keep them separated, not even death. What Poseidon had failed to mention was that the berries were highly toxic, and it would only be a few hours from eating the berries before death would find its way to the consumer's doorstep. Poseidon was confident he could convince his brother to destroy the bond once the two lovers were separated. He wanted to ensure that Atargatis would not suspect him of misdeeds which required silence from Adad. He knew the berries would result in his death shortly after consuming the berries but wanted to ensure that Atargatis would never find out about the exchange.

Adad ate the berries that evening and sat along the beach, staring dreamily at the moon. It wasn't long until Atargatis came upon him. She was surprised to see him so soon, but the surprise thrilled her. Her heart gently ached as he left for the pastures of Assyria. Like a piece of her went missing when he was gone. He smiled warmly at her and gave her a deep kiss. It was more intense than any kiss she had ever received from him before. His lips tasted of the sea. One kiss slipped into another, and another, until they were making love on the beach under the full moon. Atargatis had never felt so complete as she had that night. Her passion had never felt so fulfilled, and as she rested her head on Adad's chest in post-coital bliss, she ascended into slumber to the gentle drumming of his heart.

When daylight came, she awoke in as much bliss as she had been the night before and pulled herself up. She kissed Adad's lips. The kiss did not stir him, and his mouth tasted sour, no longer carrying the taste of the sea upon him. She nudged him to wake up. Nothing happened. Her nudge turned into a shove as tears started to escape her lids. Adad lay there, dead. She held him close as her tears grew, spilling into the sea and raising the tide. She sat there, unable to relinquish his cold, lifeless body. As morning slipped into the afternoon, she held him close. It was early evening when Poseidon came casually strolling up to them. He was a vibrant black stallion. When he saw Atargatis and the cold, stiffening body that used to be Adad, his eyes filled with concern.

"What happened?" He neighed. Atargatis pulled her eyes from Adad's face and looked at the horse that loomed over her.

"I don't know. We fell asleep on the beach last night, and when I awoke, he was like this." She pulled Adad's body closer to her bosom as if trying to warm the lifeless body up.

"Did you two kiss last night?" the stallion asked. She nodded while a new flurry of tears escaped her.

"Amongst other things," Poseidon scowled, but it went unnoticed.

"Well, that is the problem, I suppose." Atargatis looked up to him with confusion washing over her lament.

"You are a goddess, he a mortal," Poseidon continued. "The power of a kiss from a god can make a mortal man's heart burst with ecstasy." Atargatis' face twisted as she processed that information.

"He is dead because of me?" she questioned. Poseidon nodded and then shook his head, tsking as he looked at the body in her arms.

"Is there anything I can do for you, Atargatis?" She buried her face in Adad's chest as she shook her head no. Poseidon shuffled his feet and replied,

"I'm going to head out, but if you need anything, just call, and I will be there." Atargatis grabbed his hoof and squeezed it.

"Thank you," she whispered, but her tone was empty with hints of sullen comprehension. Poseidon once more nodded his head and sauntered into the sea. His look of concern morphed into a devilish smile. Atargatis would be his.

Atargatis held Adad's body for three days before some mortals came across her. They pulled her off his body. In those three days, she became increasingly more disheveled, and though even in this state, she was still exceptionally charming, there was an air about her that the mortals wanted to escape. They must have known that it was because of her that he was dead, she assumed. A funeral spire was made, and a service was held. No human had blamed her for his death, but she did, and that was enough. When all was said and done, she aimed to walk into the sea and drown herself.

Poseidon had been watching her for the days after Adad's death waiting for his opportunity to have her. He was not a patient man and was assembling a plan to drive her into his arms.

'Atargatis would be his,' he chanted on repeat within his thoughts. She just needed another push. Much to his surprise, she showed up on the banks where she and Adad spent their last night and walked into the sea. As the waves overpowered her, she did not fight them.

How lucky was he that she would come running straight to him? He smiled smugly. He would have her. She walked into the sea until her head was fully submerged. Poseidon flashed in anger. He saw that she was trying to kill herself and escape his grasp. He would have her. There would be no escape. She was in his land now, and she was his. She would find no peace because that is how he willed it.

In his wrath, her legs merged and became a tail. Her lungs flooded with water as gills emerged in her sides, and oxygen once more filled her lungs as she found breath, not in the crisp air she had been accustomed to but by processing the oxygen within the water. She had regained life in the water but why? All she wanted was to follow Adad into the depths of the underworld. Poseidon swam to her. His face twisted in anger. She was surprised that he was there and confused about what was happening. Poseidon grabbed her wrist and pulled her further into the depths of the sea.

He had pulled her further and further down until there was only darkness. It was pitch black, and she was terrified as the abyss became absolute in its shadows. She tried to pull herself away from his firm grasp, but his hold only became tighter.

"What are you doing?" Her tone was panicked and frightened. Poseidon said nothing as he pulled Atargatis further into the ocean's abyss. Finally, her wrist was released as she propelled forward, hitting the ground with so much force it knocked all air from her. She gasped at the water that contained the means to breathe. Once more, she said to the nothingness,

"What's going on?" Silence filled the darkness. Was she alone? She couldn't see anything, so she crawled on the ground, feeling her surroundings, trying to escape anywhere. Her fear consumed her panic.

From out of the darkness, a boisterous, angry voice reached her ears.

"A bottom feeder. I should have guessed." The tone of the voice gave her goosebumps and bathed her with more fear than she knew herself capable of. She began sobbing as a hand grabbed her by her throat, making her choke on her tears and fear.

"You are mine!" The voice bellowed as she became pinned and her womanhood violated. She cried for help in the darkness, but nothing was around to save her. Nothing but black, and every twist she gave in hopes of escape only pinned her deeper into the ground, and then there was nothing.

Nothing but her tears echoing into the darkness, grief-stricken and a body consumed in pain. Once he got off her, he said in a somewhat distant nonchalant voice,

"Now that you are mine, there is no reason for you ever to love another man again. Just to make sure, I'll tell you this once, your voice heard by any mortal will entrance them and bring them to madness before it results in their death." He chuckled, obviously pleased with himself.

"So stick around because escape will be so much worse." He left out the cave's opening, and she could hear a clamor suggesting her imprisonment despite his threat. She wished for death, but death was not to be her fortune.

Chapter 2: The Darkness

It felt like an eternity from when Atargatis was submerged in the darkness. She had been sobbing since she first entered this void. Her eyes hurt as if she had run dry of tears but not on the need to cry.

'At least she didn't have to worry about dry eyes as she was now submerged in water.' she thought. She could not understand how drastically her life had changed. Her happiness was an ever-fading memory. A life that, as time eroded her, felt more like a fictional concept than her past. Above her, at the water's surface, the land of man began to notice the tides shifting more. When she had tears to give, the ocean would swell, and a surge of water would grasp at the land, trying to escape as she could only dream.

She explored her surroundings blindly, touching anything and everything around her. With time she had begun to adapt to her sorrows, the darkness that ate her, and the mechanics of a tail instead of legs. Once in a while, she would be pinned and her body ravaged. There was no delicacy in Poseidon's touch. His acts upon her skin held no love but only entitlement. He has stripped away the humanity of the goddess, and she had become an empty vessel. A part of her knew she deserved the punishment she received because her love killed Adad. He would likely be alive if she had kept him at a distance, a platonic friendship. Sadly, she pursued her passion. She had sealed it with a kiss, and that kiss was his demise. So she received her punishment at the whims of Poseidon, and after the first few attacks, she no longer fought him.

As she adapted, she found herself in a cave with a gated opening. The cave was deep, and she had hoped it would lead her to the underworld, but it stopped shy of it. It was what she expected. Still, she fed on the hope that one day she would find herself again and unite with her love. If only to beg his forgiveness. She sustained herself on what she hoped was kelp. And after time passed, her eyes adapted to the dark. She wished she hadn't because now she could see Poseidon closing in on her. So she would squeeze her eyes shut and pull what was left of her psyche deep within her until he was done and gone. After she thought she was safe, she would approach the gate to explore it just in case he forgot to lock her in. Time was endless in the cave. There were no days that passed, only periods between sleep and sobs. The tide rolled in and out depending on how many tears she could expend.

One day after her punishment dealt by the hands of Poseidon, something changed. An angler fish approached her cave. Its light was abrasive to the darkness she had come to know. She kept her distance from the illumination, but upon seeing it, a feeling she had assumed she would never feel again bubbled to her surface and caught in her throat, forcing her to choke on the tears and wailing that had become her way of life. The light brought a different kind of sorrow, and she welcomed it.

She was surprised that the fish was accompanying another. Though the light's shadows made the world look hollow, she could see it was a woman. Even with the illusion of hallowed features, the lady was enchantingly beautiful. Her eyes also held a sorrow that Atargatis had grown to recognize all too well. The angelic face smiled at her, and she could feel a warmth she had thought she had forgotten. The lady had something in her hand, and she plunged her hand recklessly into an opening of the gate. It was apparent she did not fear Atargatis. In her hand was a small basket of food. Upon realizing it, Atargatis yanked it from the woman's hands and shoved bits into her mouth. It was at this moment she realized how hungry she had been. She had no desire to taste and barely chewed the food before swallowing it. She did that with each bite until there was nothing left.

She realized the food might have been intended to share only after nothing was left.

"I'm sorry," she said in a low ashamed voice.

"I didn't realize I was so hungry" Atargatis slinked away from the light. Though she liked the warmth it brought to her heart, she had grown so accustomed to the darkness that it had become harsh to her eyes. To think that once upon a time, she could bathe in the sun, and now she could barely stand this tiny little light. She reminded herself that that was a different life.

The woman laughed loudly and unabashed. The loud noise startled Atargatis, and she slid deeper into the cave. The woman seeing this adjusted her composure. Her tone was gentle and melodic.

"I see you are Poseidon's newest toy. He always forgets to feed his pets. I'm actually surprised that you've survived. Most women drown within a matter of hours." The woman paused and made a gesture in her direction.

"Well, I guess you aren't human now, are you?" Atargatis looked down at the tail she now had.

"I guess not," she replied in a defeated and mournful tone.

"Well, I am Amphitrite. It seems like just yesterday, I, too, was in that cave. The cave was built for me." Her tone was playful and sounded eerily boastful.

"And you escaped?" Atargatis tried to swallow the hope in her voice. Amphitrite laughed, and in that laugh, Atargatis felt madness seeping from the woman.

"No, of course not. I married him. When he first asked for my hand, I declined. He is a man who isn't accustomed to the word 'no,' and so I fled to save myself his wrath. A stupid dolphin found me and escorted me to that cave where I stayed until I said yes. Once I was bound to him, he let me go. Now it's all water under the bridge." she mused.

"Given enough time, I'm sure he'll get bored, and your imprisonment will end." Atargatis's heart fluttered. There may be an end to her suffering. She could barely dream of such a thing. The women continued to get to know each other with small talks about mundane and exceptional topics, but Atargatis couldn't retain any of it. She could only think that eternity could end, as could her suffering. Amphitrite left for the night, promising to return with more food and conversation and with it hope.

Over the next few months, Amphitrite would come regularly. Sometimes they would share some exotic bottle of fluid. They would talk about life before Poseidon ruled every aspect of them. Sometimes Amphitrite would come to her agitated with a constant eye over her shoulder. She supposed that although Amphitrite was out of the cage, she was still a prisoner. Atargatis looked forward to her arrival every moment she was awake. Even when Poseidon arrived, Atargatis would close her eyes, knowing her friend would likely show up when he had gone. Her body was changing, and as she adapted to each change, she found a new kind of excitement. An excitement she desperately wanted to share with her friend, but she wanted to be sure of her future before inviting anyone else into it. Then one day, Amphitrite didn't show up. The following was the same and as the moments between sleep piled up without a visit, with Aphitrite's absence, her days returned to endless.

As time did not wait for companionship, Atargatis had to find new methods of entertainment and began honing the skills she had when she was a carefree goddess. She would forage for anything that may have found itself in her cave, and with it, she would try to make little improvements in her life. Not for herself. She had stopped living for herself the moment she felt her belly swell. It was then she knew that she was with a child. She once more had a purpose. Her main concern had become masking her growing belly. She could think of countless reactions to Poseidon learning of it, but none were acceptable. She knew he would not take kindly for her disposition because, in the most bottomless pits of her heart, she knew that Adad was the father. A glimmer of a past that was gone. A ripple that she could cherish with all of herself. So she stuck barnacles to her belly and tangled her body in kelp—anything to hide her treasure from her captive.

The birth was an easy one. Atargatis kept the amiable baby deep within the cave as she feared the wrath of Poseidon. Exacerbated by the thought that the child was not his. He would bellow her name when he arrived at the cave, a new habit that she was thankful for. Her name was always said in a tone of annoyance and disgust. She would rush to the front of the cave and would accept her punishment, whatever it may be, letting him do whatever he wished to her. It didn't matter anymore. With her child close, she was revitalized, and nothing could hurt her anymore. Instead, she would come to him cowardly and small, and as he inflicted his wrath, she would leave her body making no noises of pain. When he wasn't fornicating with her, he would find amusement in hurting her in some fashion, and if she cried out, he would punish her for it. Her pain was always his pleasure. When he was satiated, he would leave, and she would weep. She had become exceptional in wound care, and as she healed her body, she would compose herself and return to the darkest depths of the cave to be reunited with her child. The child in her arms filled her with love. Looking at her, she would think about Adad, and the pain of missing him would not hurt like it once did. She still cried for him often, but the coo of her child would invigorate her, and she found a bit of peace.

One day Amphitrite returned much to the joy of Atargatis. She had missed their talks, company, and stories of a life she could now only dream of. It was her way of living vicariously. Now, for the first time in their friendship, she also had a life of her own to share. After reconnecting, she leaned close to the gate.

"Can you keep a secret?" Her voice was louder than a whisper but still hushed. Atargatis knew it was unlikely anyone was around, but she needed to protect the information. Amphitrite had an amused look on her face.

"I can keep that and so much more" Atargatis beckoned Amphitrite to stay at the gate as she delved deep into the cave. When she returned, she moved slowly and was hesitant as she closed in on the light the Angler fish accompanying Amphitrite exuded. Once in the glow emanating from the fish, Atargatis was erect, carrying a bundle of seaweed in her arms. She locked eyes with Amphitrite and beamed. Amphitrite was not impressed until the ball of seaweed cooed. Curiosity filled her hollow features. As Atargatis continued her approach, a child came into view.

"I call her Semiramis." she gently cooed to the child in her arms.

"I know she was the last gift from my beloved Adad. I just know it!" Her eyes shone as she met Amphitrite's. Amphitrite's face went sullen.

'A child,' she thought. 'This creature, whom her husband took everything from, was finding happiness.

Happiness, despite her bars, despite the atrocities brought on by her husband, was cultivating a family.'

The thought sickened her. She had begun her visitations initially out of jealousy. Her husband was a philanderer. That was no secret. He had brought this woman home to his land, and upon entering the sea, she not only gained the ability to breathe in the treacherous waters, but she morphed into a part of a fish. She had no doubt that her husband had everything to do with that. Then he locked this woman in a cell. Not just any cell, It was HER cell that he had kept her in, and that infuriated Amphitrite. Then Poseidon welcomed himself in her often, always returning. The jealousy had consumed her.

She had initially gone to check out the atrocity he had brought to her doorstep and kill her as she had done to many of his previous lovers. She knew all of his hiding spaces. Typically, she would remove any air bubbles that protected those lovers and take delight as they struggled for air only to find water. It was her favorite pastime. She had been sought after, chased by Poseidon, but it wasn't long until he took another lover. She had felt slighted back then, and his first lover was killed by accident. She didn't realize that her entry to their space would remove the air that kept them safe. She was jealous and hurt, but she knew then that it wasn't her fault the captive was in that situation. The first girl she wanted to help escape. When she entered their space, the air bubble vanished, and she panicked, trying to pull the girl to the surface. That girl didn't make it, and a part of her just said

'Good riddance' and washed her mistake clean.

After that, she began to make a habit of it. If her husband could do what he wanted with them, then it was her right to be able to do the same, being his wife. So she would compile a basket of scraps and show up as their savior. Then pop their bubble and watch their faces change from joy at the thought that they would be saved to panicking as water encompassed them. Some would reach for her, their eyes pleading for help, and then their face twisted in fear before becoming blank. She would feel satiated in her jealousy and return to her throne. She never removed their bodies but left them for Poseidon to find, like a cat leaving a dead mouse on their master's doorstep. She didn't know if he knew of her part in his concubine's demise, but whether he did or not, one thing was clear. He didn't care. For him, a woman was replaceable.

She had intended the same the first time she appeared before Atargatis. Only to be surprised to find she could breathe in the water.

'A hiccup, but death can come easy,' she thought, so it was no matter. It was the way Atargatis grabbed the food scraps, shoving them in her mouth without thought, with complete trust. Amphitrite found satisfaction in Atargatis' groveling, so she often visited to watch Atatgatis in perpetual misery. Atargatis had no desire for Poseidon. Her affections were dead and in her past. She would spend hours listening to her talk about what was. Watching the pain twist in her eyes as she recalled a time she had peace, aware that she would never have it again.

So Amphitrite would assemble a basket of food. Food that she found disgusting and would revel in watching this lowly prisoner lap it up like she had been given the most royal feast. The only quality item she ever provided to Atargatis was the drink which was only because they often would share it. Amphitrite bathed in Atargatis's subservient gratitude and would return home knowing there was only pain without her generosity.

Now Atargatis had found her light in the darkness, and that thought twisted in Amphitrite's disgust. This hope needed to end. Her voice was distant, as if recalling a memory she couldn't quite grab as she stated,

"Well, that won't do." As soon as the words escaped Amphitrite's lips, Atargatis froze. She saw a flicker of fear in Atargatis's eyes, and it became clear how Amphitrite would remedy this situation. A smile began to cross her face, and she quickly swallowed it.

"She can't stay here. What kind of life would she have behind those bars? If Poseidon realized that you had a child and, worse, that it wasn't his? She would be sacrificed instantly." Amphitrite feigned concern tsking at the thought, and terror began to seep into Atargatis's face.

"Let me take her," Amphitrite cooed. "I can give her a good life, and Poseidon is so self-involved he wouldn't even notice another child running around. He only ever notices our eldest and only boy, Triton." She couldn't help but say his name with pride. Triton was the son who was everything they could have ever wanted.

Atargatis held Semiramis closer to her. Pushing her deep into her bosom. Letting her child go would be the equivalent of giving away all of her hopes, dreams, and light. It would require a sacrifice that she was not prepared to pay, but there was truth in Amphitrite's words. Eventually, Poseidon would notice the child; if he ever found himself, not the father, her daughter would surely die. It was also known that the life she would be able to provide would be nothing but darkness. A darkness that she had become accustomed to, but her child had an opportunity for more. With her sacrifice of the joy her daughter brought to her, her daughter could possibly even see the sun. How could she deprive her love of such a thing? She began to cry, and it was clear to Amphitrite that the choice had been made. Atargatis would once more be without joy. She handed the child over, and Amphitrite assured her that they would visit, but she could never tell Semiramis of her origins as no matter the age, she would be in danger of Poseidon's wrath.

When Amphitrite returned to the palace, she looked down at the child and scowled.

"Semramis" The name rolled around in her mouth, filling it with disgust. "What an awful name. It will not do." She eyeballed the child. "You are now, Nixi. Yes," she nodded confidently. "That name will do." Amphitrite never returned to visit Atargatis; instead, she would look at Nixi and be filled with delight, thinking of the misery and darkness that Atargatis indeed found herself in. She had entertained the thought of discarding the child but enjoyed looking at her because it reminded her of Atargatis' suffering. She raised Nixi as her grandmother. She did not want to claim motherhood on something she considered beneath her. So it was rumored that although Amphitrite wore the title of grandmother, it was more likely the product of her discretion with someone other than her husband. Poseidon did not mind whether the rumor was valid as long as the children in the palace were not his problem. For each additional child Amphitrite brought home, the talk would once more be discussed in hushed tones until the story became a stale topic. She soon took two other children, Despoine and Kymopoleia, of varying ages. Both were Poseidon's love children, which Amphtrite found some value in. However, she took these children unbeknownst to any family they may have had.

Atargatis waited patiently for their return, but it never occurred. She put her energy into magic manipulations, hoping that she would, at least, one day be able to watch her beloved child grow from a distance. As time progressed, Poseidon visited less and began to leave the gate unlocked, eventually never returning to her. He likely found a new person to partake in. Atargatis felt relief as much as she felt guilt, knowing that someone else was at his mercy. She didn't leave the cave when she had been granted freedom, or at the least, forgotten. The walls held comfort for her. It was the only remnant of her child she had left. She dreamed of watching her child grow, happy and healthy, given a life that Atargatis would not have been able to provide. She harnessed her power and, as time progressed, made a name for herself as a 'fixer.' She relinquished her title as she shed her tragic past and embraced her new moniker, The Sea Witch.

Chapter 3: Nixi

Nixi's eyes opened enthusiastically when she awoke. Today was the day, and nothing could contain her excitement. She got up and shook her tail in an exuberant back-and-forth action, propelling her forward faster than usual. She first went to a shelf in her room with an assortment of conches, sea snails, and dead coral. Her brow furrowed as she examined each item before picking up a sea snail with a brown shell covered in white dots and a piece of coral with a pinkish hue. She placed both in her hair, and after a bit of fuss, the coral was tangled within her strands as the snail roamed the crown of her head. She then made her way to the feeding station. Her brother and several sisters were already feasting on various fish and vegetation. There was often a revolving number of siblings in the feeding station as her father had many progenies. Many lake and river nymphs would meander to the castle to visit each other. Some came to request an audience with Poseidon, but the wait could take months and even years for the privilege. Some would never get to be in the presence of the king of the seas. It was common knowledge that you increased the likelihood of seeing him if you came with a tribute which was often where most of the food Nixi ate came from.

Nixi beamed as she picked an eel from the coral that grew in the center of the room and placed its face into her mouth. She was always mindful of making her first bite one that killed her food. She didn't like the idea of an animal dying slowly, watching itself be consumed. The eel was exquisite today, but she was still determining if the meal was exceptional or if her excitement made everything taste better. She scanned the room, looking for Rhodos, but she didn't see her in that room. Maybe she had yet to awaken. Nixi gathered a handful of foods that she knew Rhodos would like and was about to leave the room to quest for her sister when Kymopoleia piped up with her little voice,

"Happy Birthday, Nixi!" Several others joined in on the sentiment, and the noise from it was much like she imagined a wave sounded like. She turned and scanned the room, waving to no one specific but making sure she waved in all the directions that voices had come from before resting her eyes on Kymopoleia. Nixi's smile grew and was met with an equally enthusiastic smile in return.

Nixi quickly exited the room before getting caught in a conversation like a tuna caught in a net. Usually, she would relish her time in the feeding station because she could hear tales from all the creatures that passed through. However, today was her one hundred-eightieth birthday, and with that badge of honor, she was allowed to break the surface and spy on the world of man. She wasn't allowed to go to the surface until this moment, but she must be accompanied by someone older to learn the rules of the surface world. Rhodos had accepted the request of joining the young merchild to the surface. Nixi could not be patient as her excitement demanded to be on their way. She barged into Rhodos' dwelling area only to find her still asleep. Nixi began to clatter things around in hopes of waking Rhodos, to no luck. So she got louder until she could be subtle no more, and she grabbed Rhodos, shaking her until Rhodos's eyes shot open, alert and confused. Once Rhodos accessed the information in her slumber stupor, she pushed Nixi away with a scowl.

"Get off me! Can't I just get some sleep?" She rolled out of her makeshift bed, grumbling obscenities as her body became increasingly more awake. She eyed the food in Nixi's arms taking several different kinds of fish and vegetation and began placing it in her mouth at a slow and leisurely pace.

Nixi squirmed in anticipation. "Can you hurry? We have places to be!" Rhodos glared at her half-sister and looked her up and down. You aren't even ready, so quit bugging me!" Nixi's breath deflated. What did she mean she wasn't prepared? It had been at least a year of her building up the anticipation to make the trip. Of course, she was ready! Rhodos eyed her as if listening to Nixi's thoughts.

"Look," she said in an almost inaudible growl." It is at least two days to get to land and three to get to land worth seeing. You do want to see a human right?" Nixi shook her head yes enthusiastically.

"Then you'll need more food for traveling, and you will also need a weapon for hunting." She continued.

"I am not in charge of feeding or keeping you alive. I am going to make sure you don't get caught. Humans can be pretty mean to our kind, so we keep ourselves hidden. I am going to teach you how to do that. This isn't a pleasure excursion. This is education." Rhodos erected herself confidently as the idea of being a mentor and teacher filled her with pride. She was always a studious type, but she had an overwhelming passion for sharing knowledge. Nixi smiled at the thoughts knowing her sister was only grumpy about her abrupt awakening.

“Go get some hunting gear from Triton and tell him to get ready." Nixi looked confused.

"What is he getting ready for?" Rhodos signed loudly and slammed the freshly shucked shells she had been fiddling with down.

"Just go get him!" snapped Rhodos. Nixi quickly exited the room, fearing being there any longer would only result in things being thrown at her.

She then found herself in the doorway of Triton's room. She was surprised that he had planned to join them in her adventure. He was a stoic type and was often unavailable. He often was, with his father, being, the right hand of Poseidon. After all, Triton was the one that would inherit it all if his father ever decided to relinquish the throne. It was because of this that he rarely was available for social events. Nixi gently tapped on his door, and his cold gaze wandered to it and rested on Nixi. She smiled brightly, but there were no emotions returned her way.

"Is it time to go?" His voice was somber and haunting. Nixi loved hearing his voice, and some of her best memories were of him telling a tale to her as she drifted off to sleep.

"Almost!" she piped, a drastic change to his voice. "Rhodos is getting ready and told me I needed a weapon for hunting. Do you have anything I could use?" Triton made no comment but went to a corner of his room and pulled his hunting gear across his body. Then, as if barely a thought, he grabbed a bit of a net lying on the ground and a small piece of whalebone and tossed it in her direction. The bone had been carved, and an intricate design lay across one side. The carving had a mermaid etched across the handle with her name down the side. The other side of the bone had been whittled into a sharp point, and it was obvious that it was a knife that he had made specifically for her. He had never given her anything that would constitute a gift before. She held it close, and he approached her. He was significantly larger than her. His build was similar in size to some whales she had seen, and he loomed over her who, at best, was the size of a shark or a porpoise. He adjusted the net on her body and secured a place to hold the intricately fashioned blade.

"I'll meet you both out front in a little bit" He gently pushed Nixi backward and then closed his door in her face so the door brushed her nose.

'That was so weird,' she thought as her fingers drifted to her new blade. 'It was so cool!' She rarely got to spend time with him, but now she would get to spend a few days with him. How thrilling! She bobbed to the castle entrance, smiling at both strange and familiar visitors. After about thirty minutes, Rhodos sauntered over to her. Her face was more pleasantly amused than earlier. Nixi exhaled in joy. She had been worried that Rhodos would have a mood the entire trip. As Trition joined them, she became serious in attitude, fearing they would change their minds; she kept quiet and followed her two older siblings. Without their agreement to come, she would not get to see the sea's surface. It would soon be time to see her first human, and she could not wait.

Chapter 4: Breaking the Surface

Nixi was tired. She and her siblings had been swimming all day, and her excitement and enthusiasm had washed away. They hadn't even gone to the surface to peek at the world above her own. She wanted to complain, and if it had only been her and Rhodos, she would have begged and pleaded until her sister submitted to her desires, but Triton was not as easy of a target. Too much pressure from her, and they would be returning to the kingdom, and she might never get to see the surface world. She wished he hadn't decided to join them. Her body ached, and Triton wasn't particularly fond of breaks, so she was relieved when Rhodos demanded he halt—explaining how his swim span was double that of either of them. Rhodos was almost as small as Nixi, so she was likely just as tired as she was. It wasn't until Triton agreed to stop for the night that Nixi finally released a breath of air she had been holding in anticipation. When Nixi approached Rhodos, who had already spread out on a rock looking relaxed and leisurely, she turned to Nixi and grinned.

"What are you doing?" Nixi looked at her on the rock gesturing that she would follow suit.

"You still have to gather some food for us." Nixi's confused expression twisted into unsure defiance. She had never had to forage, let alone hunt for food. Everything had always been supplied in the feeding station, and now, for some arbitrary reason, she had been elected to feed not just herself but the whole party. She tried to protest, but it was stopped short by Triton firmly patting her back.

"C'mon," he grumbled, "I'll show you some basics."

The three of them were no longer at the bottom of the ocean but instead close to a cliff that had a sharp drop-off into some unknown depth. Triton pushed Nixi forward.

"You don't want to hunt in the wide open ocean. The best places are closer to the ground. The deeper into the sea depths you go, the more the fish will taste weird, and the harder the hunt becomes." She slinked back until she fell behind her brother, following him, only casually listening to him.

"There are five pelagic zones. Hadopelagic, which you will never need to visit. Those that live in it are basically gatekeepers of Hades. The Abyssopelagic, equally useless to you, and then the Bathypelagic zone, where the kingdom you grew up in is. However, It is the

Mesopelagic zone that has the best and safest hunting" Triton spun around, making his eyes equal hers.

"Never, never hunt any higher than two hundred meters. Anything higher than two hundred meters in depth is for man and carries too much risk for your type. Hunting in those waters almost guarantees getting caught in a net and dying."

"How do I know I'm too high?" Nixi said in a cautious tone.

"That's easy. There is a change in the water pressure and temperature for each barrier." As he said, she was hit with a wave of warmth and lightness. The air felt thinner and made her dizzy. Triton looked at her as she let out a gasp. A smile slipped across his face. "Nixi, welcome to the hunting grounds."

As she caught her breath, she saw they were at a clearing. There were animals scuttling on its bottom and a variety of fish she had not seen before swimming across it. Some fish swam toward her, curious, only to dart away when she moved.

"Get out your knife," Triton commanded. She pulled her blade out of the net it was being carried in.

"See that cliff?" He gestured to a rock formation that had holes placed all over it. "That is where the easiest prey is. All you need is patience."

They hovered outside the cliff, and Triton became still. Nixi mimicked him. She found staring at a cliff boring, but she was excited to spend time with her brother. She didn't think they had ever been alone before, and as she explored the thought, an eel popped its head out and grabbed a fish that had been casually swimming by. Nixi jumped in surprise.
Triton looked at her and then at the hole.

"Now you go after it" He shoved Nixi forward and then instructed her to stick her hand in the hole to pull the eel out and stab it in the face. Nixi did as told and, through a lot of struggle, eventually grabbed the wolf eel and pulled it out of its hole, stabbing it in the face until it stopped moving. Triton patted her on the back.

"Good job!" Nixi had hunted an eel! She had impressed herself. She then spent the rest of the evening reenacting the story to Rhodos until they had all fallen asleep.

The next morning Triton woke Nixi up early and requested she follow him. In her sleepy haze, she swerved while trying to keep up with her brother. He shot up, and she struggled to follow. As she pushed on, the temperature and pressure changed, and the water began to change colors. She had wanted to look at the changes but was determined to do her best to keep up with him, and then he stopped. She could not slow down, and before she knew it, her body was exposed to a new sensation as she propelled past the ocean's surface. She felt weightless momentarily and then very heavy as her face slapped back into the water. Triton roared with laughter.

He then showed her how to peek only her eyes out of the water so she could breathe and watch a ball of fire pull over the horizon and set in the morning sky. Telling Nixi the history of the sun, a chariot pulling across the sky who had married their sister. They then returned to Rhodos, who had finally awoken and gathered her things, ready to start the day anew. They swam once more for the entirety of the day, but Nixi was tired and swam slowly. So Triton had her grab him, dragging her so she could keep up. Once more, she hunted with little success. Triton reassured her that she would never have to go hungry with practice.

Triton was gone when she awoke the following day, but Rhodos was awake much earlier than expected.

"Triton wouldn't be with us," she told Nixi, "Today would be the day to explore a city." Nixi was ready to bounce for joy, but the increased enthusiasm caused Rhodos to bark orders about not being allowed to be seen. Rhodos demanded obedience, stating that the trip would be over if Nixi couldn't follow instructions. Nixi agreed, as there was nothing else she could do. The two swam upward, and Nixi noted they were close to the surface. Light shone through the water, and Nixi played in the strip of the sun's rays, causing warm and cold waters. She also saw the hulls of ships and explored them, eating some sea bugs and gathering others in Nixi's net for later. It wasn't until that evening that Nixi and Rhodos made it into the harbor.

Chapter 5: A City Discovered

The harbor boats moved so much that Nixi was immediately entranced. Rhodos picked some barnacles from a passing ship and rapidly popped them into her mouth. They were small and had a crunch to them. They were a spectacular snacking food. She cut a bit of net hanging in the water and placed several more in it so she had a bag to swim around with, casually munching while giving a general tour. Nixi had never had a barnacle before and approached the ship's hull, picking it off the boat and timidly putting it in her mouth. She bit down on it, which made a loud crunch as it collapsed between her teeth, releasing a buttery taste.

'This is excellent!' she thought and grabbed her travel bag greedily, shoving barnacles into it. Her sister

Despoine would love it, and it would be a great gift to share with her if she didn't eat them all on the journey back.

Rhodos swam to the harbor floor, waving for her sister to follow. When Nixi got to the sea bed, she saw a basket with a crustacean trapped in it.

"They call this a portumnus latipes" She opened the basket and removed the crap-like creature tossing a rock in its wake and closing it again. She then split the creature in two, handing half of it to Nixi. It was also delicious but less exciting than the barnacles. She had had crustaceans before, although she was unsure if she had ever had this species. "I always put a rock in exchange for food just in case the humans noticed that something had been captured before."

Rhodos swam over to an opening in the harbor.

"This is the island of Rhodes." Rhodos puffed out her chest, proud to show off an island named after her.

"It is where I met Helios, and we first joined in union." She gave a lavish sigh as she recalled the moments shared with her husband. Nixi looked up and saw people.

"Do not let yourself be seen under any circumstances," Rhodos demanded. Nixi absentmindedly nodded in agreement as she watched the humans go about their day from the comfort of the bottom of the river. The humans were loud and busy, but she was excited to see fabrics as she peeked at someone doing their laundry nearby. She saw people walking along the river, some looking happy and having a leisurely gait and others quicker, more determined to get wherever they were going. A large fellow was eating a fowl of some kind tossing his refuse into the river. Nixi couldn't help herself and put a bit of the strange food in her mouth. The bit of chicken tasted burnt and ashy.

"This is what humans eat? How awful!" She was thankful not to be a human at that moment. Rhodos chuckled.

As they continued down the river, Rhodos would occasionally point at something and give a little speech recounting the history of the place in her best tour guide voice. There was so much to take in that often Nixi couldn't choose a direction to look in as she feared missing anything. It wasn't until she got to a bridge that she stopped whipping her eyes from one thing to another. After noticing her sudden fixation, Rhodos began explaining bridges droning on about their construction. It, however, was not what Nixi was looking at. In the center of the bridge was a man with long hair leaning on the guard rail, absently looking out at the river and possibly even gazing at the sea. He had long blonde hair that brushed his cheek in the wind and a face with sharp features. Nixi could not recall seeing anything more beautiful than he.

As if he felt her eyes on him, he stopped leaning against the wall and stood erect. Another man said something, and he turned to him. He smiled at the man, and Nixi felt a nauseating twist in her stomach. Was this a swoon? Is this what swooning was? She then remembered that Rhodos was with her. Rhodos had stopped speaking, and Nixi was unsure for how long, so she turned to her to say,

"I think that's weird but also really ingenious." She glanced back at the man who was now moving off the bridge. She casually meandered in the same direction as he, stopping to ask about something in the area he occupied anytime he stopped. She knew if she mentioned the man, Rhodos would likely yell at her, so they casually stalked him until he went beyond where he could be seen.

After he left, she no longer enthusiastically looked at anything. Her heart ached at his missing presence. When Rhodos questioned her about it, she said she was tired and likely needed a rest after so much stimulation. Rhodos agreed a break would be a good idea, so they returned to the security of the sea. Nixi was quiet on their swim back to where they were camping. Once they got there, Rhodos announced that they would return once the evening was upon them, as the nights in the square were the best part of humanity, in her opinion.

When evening came, they fed again and returned to the river a few meters from the bridge where Nixi had seen the man. There was an open area just beyond it that Rhodos called a square. The evening was a stark difference from the daytime. Most of the city was dark, except for the square, which was lit up with torches and had the people grouped in the area. A roar of chatter came from it, and occasionally a laugh would pierce through the night. It was a festive and happy occasion, and the fires that lit up the area were just as pretty as her first look at the stars.

Rhodos tapped on Nixi's shoulder to get her attention.

"The coolest thing about the night is that people won't see you as long as you follow a few rules. One, stay in the dark spots of the river. The second is you can pop your head out but keep your nose and mouth under water. That way, you can breathe. Third, make sure there are no humans that might see your head in the water. Easy as that!" Rhodos first broke the surface, her eyes floated just above the water line, and Nixi mimicked her position. She did not struggle with the move as she had with Trition and mentally thanked him for the practice. Rhodos was on edge today and would likely end the night tour if Nixi was more trouble than Rhodos had the energy for.

Upon breaking the surface, the world above the water was more vivid. There was a distortion of looking at the land through the water she hadn't known about. The fire didn't dance as it did from under the surface, and the darkness was brighter than she realized. She was in awe of the sights that lay before her. She heard footsteps from the road before the bridge and saw the man from earlier that had caught her attention. He was walking with another man, and they were talking. They chuckled at some story they discussed as they emerged on the other side of the bridge approaching the square. They were about to enter the crowd when the companion of the tall blonde man mentioned he had forgotten something. The man that Nixi fixated on offered to join him in obtaining the lost item, and much to Nixi's dismay and anger, he declined. As the friend approached the bridge again, her new obsession began to walk back toward the crowd.

She knew that once he did, she was likely never to see him again, and she had to do something about it. She needed him to return to the water so she could gaze at him again. So she decided to do something drastic. She took a deep breath before shooting up, exposing her body to her shoulders, and yelled,

"Wait!" She was surprised when she almost immediately was yanked back down by Rhodos. As soon as Nixi was back underwater, Rhodos grabbed her hand and swiftly started swimming back toward the sea. Nixi didn't even get to see if her desire had heard her. She tried to break free from Rhodos, but Rhodos had a strength that, up until this moment, Nixi had never seen. The more she pulled away, the more her sister would yank her closer and increase her speed.

Shortly after they had swam under the bridge, she heard a splash. She looked at where it was coming from. When she turned around, she saw it was the associate of the blonde man. He had jumped in and was swimming toward her. However, he could not keep up with Rhodos' speed, and soon, the man was being pulled out of the water by a few men who had followed him. They pulled him out of the water in much the same way as Rhodos was escaping with Nixi. The man was fighting them, and just like her, he too was overpowered by those trying to save him.

They didn't stop in the harbor for a last snack. Rhodos still had a firm grasp on her as they passed the area they had previously stayed. It was then Nixi stopped fighting Rhodos' grip and went limp. Once she had done that, Rhodos slowed her pace, and when she found a nice clearing, she stopped, letting go of Nixi. Nixi rubbed her wrist as Rhodos spun around to face her. Rhodos had the scariest scowl Nixi had ever seen, and seeing it on such a well-tempered face somehow made it even more frightening.

"Do you know what you did?" She yelled despite being not more than a yard away. Nixi shook her head no. She knew she was in trouble for breaking the rules but didn't understand why it was such a big deal. She didn't even get to see the blonde man again.

"You didn't listen to me, you stupid jellyfish!" Rhodos' face was twisted in anger.

"Oooooo, I broke the surface," Nixi taunted. "But what's the big deal? No one saw us. They were all looking at that guy that fell in the water. No harm, no foul." Nixi shrugged.

"That GUY," Rhodos had a mocking tone as she emphasized the word 'guy,' "was in the water BECAUSE of you." Once more, highlighting the word 'because.' Nixi let out a breath of air that was steeped in tones of disbelief.

"That GUY may never recover from what you did." Rhodos' face increased in a distortion that was evident in anger. Nixi tried to protest. How could she be responsible for some random person falling into the water? Rhodos attempted to regain some degree of composure.

"You are an idiot," she exclaimed, her voice sounding tired.

'She was the idiot,' Nixi indignantly thought. All she wanted was to look at a man. How would that make her an idiot? Rhodos sat on the ocean bed and patted a spot next to her, gesturing for Nixi to sit down. Nixi did not sit down, and Rhodos looked at her with a sharpness that made Nixi's skin feel prickly. So she sat down across from her. She'd sit down but not where she was told to.

"There are reasons we have rules. I didn't think you'd act so frivolously and put people in danger. Obviously, I overestimated our relationship. You broke my trust and destroyed that man, possibly forever." Rhodos voice stopped sounding angry and instead was weary and sad.

"Humans can not see us because it increases harm to both parties. If a human sees you, they will aim to hunt you, as there are stories out there that killing merfolk can cure disease, be an aphrodisiac, and grant wishes. The stories change from place to place, but they all have one solution. To hunt and kill the merfolk. Getting caught ensures your death and puts your entire family and friends in danger. Humans can become fixated and toxic when they get an idea. They are like lagocephalus. Once you see one, you know the entire ecosystem is about to get disturbed. Possibly even forever changed. To be seen puts everyone at risk."

Rhodo's paused, finding herself out of breath from swimming so fast while pulling an indignant creature.

"Like many sea creatures, though, we have a defense system. When a human hears our voice, they become obsessed with it. So much so that they will swim for miles trying to find it until they are exhausted and drown. That man who heard you will likely always try to find you and will likely drown himself. It may be tonight or in years, but he will always try to follow your voice, and it will eventually kill him." Nixi sat there slack-jawed.

"Why wouldn't you tell me this sooner." Rhodes scoffed.

"You've been told thousands of times." Nixi began to protest that she hadn't, but before she could find the words, Rhodos cut her off.

"You've heard the story of the siren your whole life."

"A siren?" Nixi responded. "I'm not a siren. They are boogeymen, a story to convince children to behave. They are not facts." she reassured herself.

"A half human, half fish, whose song sends men to their graves. Take a look in the mirror. That IS YOU." Rhodos taunted.

"Well, I didn't sing. So that man had nothing to do with me." Rhodos sighed, and Nixi couldn't decide if it was at her or if she was tired.

"When a human hears your voice, it sounds like a song to their pathetic ears. It's a song they can not forget. If you ever need to talk to a human, talk to the extremely old. They either can't hear you or want to be dead anyway."

Rhodos got back up. We should get as far as we can tonight. Nixi began to protest. They were supposed to be looking at humans for another day. She wanted to go back and check on the blonde man one last time. Rhodos shot her a glance that felt like daggers to her throat, so she stopped the protest, sank her head, and began swimming toward home.

Chapter 6: The Return

It wasn't far on their path that they once more saw Triton, and the three of them began their journey back home. Nixi was uncharacteristically quiet when she saw him. She didn't want to get yelled at more than Rhodos had already done, but that was only a small portion of why she sought silence. Triton had always had a way of purging her secrets. He was so good at it that he didn't need to speak to her to get it. So she avoided eye contact and tried to make herself as small as possible. She was hoping to pass by her brother's watchful eye. Although she hated the idea of getting yelled at again, her more immense fear was that if she discussed it with him, it could give away that as soon as she could, she would return to that town to find the man she had not stopped thinking about. The more she fussed, the longer it would take her to be reunited with the man she so desperately wanted to see again.

Rhodos was more than happy to tell Triton about the man that had jumped into the river when she had spoken. As he heard the recounting, he became quieter. With his silence, his veneer became more prominent and more daunting. Forcing Nixi to get even smaller out of a combination of fear and shame. She hated getting in trouble with him because of his daunting personality and because he had a direct line with her father, Poseidon.

She would likely have to succumb to her father's wrath if he mentioned anything about what had happened.

Her dad was temperamental, and she tried to avoid her father's wrath when possible. The more Triton knew about her mistake, the more likely her father would also know about it. What scared her the most was anyone finding out about the man who had caught Nixi's affection. She knew now that her love for him was forbidden, and either of them would suffer if he were discovered the keeper of her heart.

When they returned home, Kymopoleia and Despoine were eagerly awaiting her arrival. Her two sisters separated her from the weary and intimidating Rhodos and Triton. She shared the barnacles she had collected on her travels and managed not to eat so her two enthusiastic sisters could try and began to tell them of all the things she had seen. She also told them with shame about the man who had jumped into the river after she had made the mistake of speaking out loud. Their eyes grew wide and rolled with laughter, much to Nixi's surprise.

Despoine was able to swallow her giggles first.

"I've had my moments with humans. Once there was a blonde boy child who I just needed to know. Every day he would come to the harbor and spend hours looking into the water. I watched him watch the water, and I lived for it. One time I got too close, and he saw me. He immediately got up and went to report what he had seen. So I asked him to stop. Which he did. He then turned around and jumped into the water. Then he started flailing about and splashing, making a ruckus, I tried to save him by giving him air, but he started to swallow the water instead. I then panicked and, trying to fix my mistake, pushed him into a shallow part of the harbor. He immediately started to go back into the deeper waters and eventually drowned. People heard, but it was too late. The boy was dead, and I had to make a break for the deep seas so that no one would hunt me down." her eyes teared ever so slightly, and she shook her head as if trying to shake off the memory. She once more smiled at Nixi.

"So don't stress it. Just learn from the experience!" She hugged Nixi, but Nixi felt it was more for Despoine than herself.

Kymopoleia joined in on the hug to comfort Despoine.

"My first experience was this time I was hanging out with some walrus friends, and we were singing. It was a pretty foggy day, so our visibility of the area was low. All of a sudden, I heard a couple of splashes. One of the guys went to check it out and informed us that a ship was nearby, and the men were jumping off it. We were curious, so several of us went to check it out. The people that had jumped in started to swim before me, and in my fear, I swam home. When I returned to the walrus colony a few weeks later, they told me the men had tried to follow me, swimming as deep as they could until they drowned. There were 5 of them. I stopped hanging out with them for years, and when I do, I visit only on clear days so I don't cause an event like that again. I still fear that if it happens again, men will hunt down the walrus colony I am so fond of."

"Is there any way to not have stuff like that happen?" Despoine and Kymopoleia laughed simultaneously.

"Of course, there is!" they exclaimed in unison. Nixi's heart leapt in excitement as she perked up, giving double her attention to her sisters. "You just don't bother with humans! Or you die. Death is the only surefire way to end the curse. You cause their death, or they cause yours." Nixi's heart sank, and she tried to cover up her disappointment at the answer.

"Humans are designed to sacrifice their lives to be with us. I heard a story that it is because of a goddess loving a man who she killed. In her shame, she became a mermaid, and that love ripple forever tore human and mer apart." Despoine said. Looking at the empty bowl of snacks, Despoine excused herself, getting up and leaving the area. Kymopoleia watched her as she exited the room and looked at Nixi, giving her a sad smile.

"That boy's death changed Despoine," Her tone grew deeper.

"I don't know if she'll ever fully recover. I think she loved that boy. So it's a dangerous game, interacting with humans. It seems you end up with one of two paths when you involve yourselves with them. You carry the heartache of hurting that which you love like us." Kymopoleia reminisced.

"Or you take joy in the slaughter of humans like Benthesikyme, who will use the waves to pull all sorts of humans and beasts out to sea, telling them to follow her to salvation where she swims ahead, watching them fight to get to her until they drown from lack of swimming skill or exhaustion. Once they have perished, she tosses the bodies upon the beach where they are destined to be found."

Nixi resolved to stay away from the man to save him from their likely destiny, but her thoughts would wander toward him daily. It had been a month since her first sight of him, and every day, her heart would break as she remembered that he could only find death with her. She had never felt alone before, but knowing she would not be able to be with him, no amount of interaction with others could stave off her loneliness. In that loneliness, she decided she would have to see him once more, if only for her to have closure over the matter. She grabbed her net satchel and knife. Then she left home searching for the town she had which held the man she could not get to leave her mind. She told no one where she was going and knew that as long as she didn't have to explain herself, no one would likely notice her absence. If they did, she could be in loads of trouble for taking the journey alone amongst the ridicule of her newfound love.

Finding the familiar harbor took her several days and two other towns. She waited for nightfall before entering the brackish waters of the river next to the square. The city was darker than the last time she was there. The bonfire that had lit up the town square was out, and the people were mostly safely tucked in their houses. Though the darkness was seeping in solitude, she was grateful. She was more comfortable in the dark than squinting through the light she was not accustomed to. Her dismay at the lack of people also seemed to mean that the man she was searching for was not to be found. A disappointment and somehow a relief. She couldn't get in too much trouble if she encountered no humans.

She loomed near the bridge where the man had fallen in hopes he would cross her path. As morning approached, she could hear the town start to awake. The dawn signaled that she needed to return to deeper waters and try once more the following night. The second night was much like the first, and her lack of success was disheartening to her. On the third night, the bonfire was lit. The people were out a bit later, so she kept to the shadows of the bridge more diligently. As the night progressed, she began to lose hope. Maybe she was not destined to see the man that had captured her heart. She knew it might be destiny keeping her from him and told herself with each passing moment that it was her last. Proceeding each vow, she would hesitate only to restart the vow of departure. When she thought she had finally caught the nerve to leave, she heard two men on the bridge conversing.

"Dorus, I wish you could understand me. I appreciate you taking me to the bridge weekly to look at the water, but I know she is waiting for me!" The man's voice cracked in distress. Leaning heavily on the bridge rail as if trying to fall through it.

"I heard her voice and knew I needed to find her immediately." A man grabbed him by his collar, pulling him away from the railing.

"Tiberus, why would you want to follow some voice in your head when you have such a loving wife and family at home? You are addicted to a fantasy of your imagination. Isn't it better to live for them than this fictitious moment you've fixated on? I was there when you claimed to have first heard that ethereal voice. There was no voice, or I would support you in this quest. I'm sorry to say that what you search for is in your head and your head alone." Tiberus sighed in exasperation.

"If it was only in my head, I cannot understand nor accept that the voice I heard is untrue. It haunts every fiber of my being. I may not have seen her, but I swear I have loved nothing more!" The second man corralled the first off the bridge, and as they escorted the other from the river, Nixi could see that the conversation was none other than the man who had jumped after her and the love for which all of this had begun. Her heart leaped at the sight of him, and she likely would have called him again if she had not heard the plights of the man who had listened to her call on her first visit.

She loved how much he cared for his friend, who was going through a difficult time. Although he looked tired, she couldn't help but find him even more attractive than when she had seen him. Dorus knocked on a door, and a woman answered it. The friend sauntered inside. That must be the man's wife, Nixi thought. Her face was puffy and red, as if she had been crying. She thanked Dorus for his watchful eye before closing the door. When the door closed, Dorus once more returned to the walkway that ran alongside the river. He looked at the water and sighed as he thought about his friend, who had become obsessed with it for no discernible reason.

He had begun doing a weekly walk with his friend after he had been caught diving into the river twice in the same month. Although he was endlessly familiar with his friend's plight, he could not understand what had happened the first night he had jumped into the river to save his friend. One moment he was okay, and the next, he was obsessed about facts that, as far as he could see, never happened. He could hear fish jumping out of the water, making playful noises as they promised successful fishing. Still, he had lost heart in fishing as now all he saw when he looked at the water was his closest friend's insanity that had flooded into Tiberius. Then he, too, turned in for the night.

Nixi had followed his every move. She desperately wanted to call out for him but feared subjecting him to the madness that had found his friend. As she followed him, she occasionally breached the water's surface to look at him. His presence was as intoxicating to her as hers was to his friend. When she would catch herself being exposed, she would quickly submerge herself back under, and every time she did, he would look in her direction, thinking it was a fish jumping. Keeping him from seeing her when she so desperately wanted to be seen by him was the hardest thing she had ever done. She watched the door when he entered his domicile until the space went dark. When she was sure he would not return to look out upon the water she lingered in, she returned home with a better understanding of her love and situation. She would gladly watch him forever, but in the knotted pit of her stomach, she knew if she stayed, she would eventually be seen, and he would be lost to her forever.

When Nixi returned home, she was not the flibbertigibbet that people were accustomed to. Her smiles were as forced as her conversation. She did not fawn over the pets that often accompanied the subjects of the sea and no longer squealed in delight when her favorite foods were found sequestered to the dining coral. There was a melancholy air about her, and although her sisters immediately noticed the change in her demeanor, they brushed it off as a lousy day until it exceeded a week. After barricading herself in her room and interacting with her friends and family at its bare minimum, her sisters were tasked with an intervention. They would find out what was going on with the youngest of them. They missed the girl they knew.

Despoine had arrived in her doorway demanding an audience of her. She had baited the demand with Benthesikyme's return. Her arrival brought a tradition of stories that Nixi was known to enjoy. Nixi initially denied the invitation, so Despoine sweetened the pot with the snacking of barnacles and a threat that if she didn't come to them, they would all find themselves in her room, and then there would be no escape. When Nixi entered the room, she noticed all her sisters were already there. Even Rhodos, who generally disliked story time, sat curled up in a corner staring at a book in a trance-like state. Kymopoleia grabbed Nixi's hand and pulled her to the floor immediately in front of Benthesikyme; she then pushed a sizeable overflowing bowl of barnacles onto Nixi's lap. Nixi looked at the bowl, and her heart sank. She remembered how buttery they tasted, but it reminded her of him. Would she always feel this void in her?

Benthesikyme began her tales. She often had the best stories as she took joy in swimming the globe, consorting with other gods to bring aid to the typhoons, hurricanes, and the off wave to bring havoc or happiness to people. She was the goddess of waves and, in being so, also had the most interactions with humans. However, she had as much compassion for humans as a wolf does for sheep. She often compared people to livestock but chose not to hunt the species for any other reason than the pleasure of it. She had drowned many by grabbing them by the ankles as she disguised herself as a wave and pulled them deep into the depths of the sea. Her indifferent thoughts on the matter of humans caused her to be the best storyteller of all of them. Her tales often were sprinkled with sex, violence, and an unapologetic air in all her actions.

When she had concluded her stories, Nixi saw an opportunity for escape. She had almost reached the doorway when the dark velvety voice of Benthesikyme caught her.

"Nixi, it's your turn to entertain us with a story. So you better not think you are bound for your room again. Her head sank as she turned around and traded spots with Benthesikyme. Nixi's shoulders dropped, and she understood that all of the evening was a ruse to get her to tell them what was on her mind. She didn't want to share her heartbreak with her siblings. She just wanted to find solitude and dream of his face. She also knew that if she didn't give them something, then they would be relentless if finding out her truth. If she talked now, she could at least be in charge of the narrative.

Recounting the discovery of barnacles, her introduction to hunting, and the bonfire. She told them about her first visit to the Isle of Rhodes. She had told them that she had thought a man was about to be attacked, so she tried to call out to him, causing another man to make her aware of the burden of knowing she was cursed. A fact that she had not been willfully privy to up until that moment. When she had finished recounting the tale, she got up and once more made her way to the door.

"What of your second visit? Why don't you tell us of it?" Nixi felt a cold, sharp hit to her heart as she heard Rhodos speak. She was slow to turn around as she recovered from the accusation and faced her with an innocent

"Hmm?" Rhodos' book snapped shut.

"I want to know what happened on your latest trip there. You were there for three days at least, and when you returned, you have been a somber shell of yourself. So I think we would all like to know what happened." The entire room nodded in agreement. She had been ambushed. Nixi knew the story time had been a trap when she was forced to actively participate, but she had thought she had passed the test with flying colors. She was dismayed that everything up until this moment had been nothing but bait, and she had been caught.

"Oh," she quietly said. "When that man jumped into the river, a new aspect of my life came to light. I learned that I shouldn't be heard nor seen. If I was, there were repercussions. That I was a key to madness for the mortal realm. I didn't understand what that meant, so I had to find out. The man still quests for the waters. He is not left unattended, and his wife cries about it often. He misses me, and yet he knows nothing about me." Her voice was low and ashamed.

"I now understand more than I once did." Then her tone changed to accusatory "Is that enough." Rhodos responded with apathetic disdain,

"It's not because you didn't talk about the man you called out to. Just a pathetic placeholder of some burglary you claim to have tried to intervene in." She chuckled,

"You act like I wasn't there to see your infatuation destroy that man's life. You are responsible for your actions. It's a shame you are feigning denial about it." Rhodos got up and diligently passed Nixi as she exited the room. Nixi waited a minute, standing there without words to respond to a moment already passed. The rest stared blankly at Nixi, awaiting a response to the accusation, but Nixi didn't want to explain herself, so she, too, exited the room and returned to her chambers.

When she finally reached her room, she crumpled on the bed in tears. An hour or so later, Benthesikyme entered her room. Nixi choked on her tears, trying to swallow the distress.

"No need to cry, my dear sister." Benthesikyme cooed as she rubbed Nixi's shoulders.

"Infatuation is hard sometimes. Thinking you love a human is… complicated" Her voice drifted dreamily to Nixi.

"You wouldn't understand," Nixi responded flatly.

"Oh, wouldn't I," her sister teased. Nixi abruptly pulled herself up so she could face her sister.

"You wouldn't because it's not infatuation, it's love." Nixi's eyes were as stern and defiant as her voice, and Benthesikyme couldn't help but laugh.

"Well, there is just one thing to do then." Nixi looked at her sister quizzically. "I guess I'll just have to see what all the fuss is about." Nixi's brow furrowed, and Benthesikyme laughed. "I'll see you in the morning; you must show me the man."

"Why?" Nixi softly questioned, swallowing her blubbering tears.

"Well, I must see what he's all about to decide if I should help you."

"Help me?" Nixi echoed. Benthesikyme patted her head as she arose.

"We will head out first thing tomorrow!" and she bounced out of the room.

The following day Nixi entered the kitchen quietly. She didn't want to discuss the night before with them, nor did she want to let on that her sister would escort her to her beloved. Three of her sisters were fawning over each other telling secrets and giggling amongst themselves. None of them noticed as Nixi glided by the room they were in. Her oldest sister, Rhodos, was once more curled up in her study, deep in thoughts that resembled a trance. When Rhodos got in such a way, her world tended to fall by the wayside, and there was rarely a success at disturbing her. Nixi knew she was going to make a clean break. She quickened her pace as she burst through the doors of the palace.

"Off to see your lad, are we?" The words cut through Nixi, paralyzing her in fear. She was busted. She turned to face Rhodos while fumbling through words. Searching for a viable excuse to be leaving the area. How could Nixi elude her perceptive sister? Benthesikyme pushed past Rhodos announcing to Nixi and the room,

"Well then, let's go." Rhodos could not hide the confusion from her face, causing Benthesikyme to laugh hysterically.

"I want to see what all the fuss is about." She turned to Nixi, "Plus, you don't get a choice. You aren't supposed to go topside alone, and if I don't come, then I'll tell Amphitrite, and you'll never get to go topside again. So me going with you is the only choice you get." Benthesikyme grinned in a way that was her signature 'I'm going to get what I want' smile.

The two of them swam toward the harbor. They could see it was a busy, sunny day from just under the surface. Benthesikyme squealed in excitement.

"There will be people at the beach today!" Nixi was unsure what that meant, but Benthesikyme had taken her hand and pulled her toward the town before she could ask. They were about half a mile from the shore, and Benthesikyme had a flicker of trouble in her eyes that worried Nixi. Benthesikyme approached the beach, where many people were wading in the waters. Nixi had never been so close to people as they swam around her. She stayed low to the floor as people floated above. Her sister was much more brazen as she swam between people tugging at their clothes so that the human briefly sank and would feverishly swim back to the surface. She would then return to Nixi's side. Laughing hard, her face was bright red, and joyous tears emerged from her eyes.

Benthesikyme grabbed her hand.

"Do you want to see something hilarious?" She asked with the same troublesome smile Nixi shook her head no, but before she could vocalize her desire to leave, Benthesikyme had swam to the surface, breaking beyond it like a stone, shattering glass. She bobbed up and down, splashing around. She flailed around for a second, and then Nixi saw several people swimming toward her. She wanted to call out for her sister to warn her, but there was no time. She swam to her sister, grabbing her tail and yanking her deep beneath the surface. Benthesikyme did not fight the tug but swam further away from the scene. Nixi chased after her, finding it hard to keep up as her heart beat faster than she had ever felt it beat before.

"So, now that the fun has been had, where is this fellow you have been fawning over?" Benthesikyme's face became somber in a way that Nixi was unfamiliar with. She had forgotten all about the man which she lived to see. Her sister's trickery had stressed her out too much to think about him. Then the thought crossed her mind that maybe this was a nefarious plan of her sister. Perhaps she wanted to see the man so that she could do something to him. Her love did not feel safe in the presence of Benthesikyme.

"How about we just go home. I'm not feeling well." Nixi said softly.

"No. No. No. No. No. We are here because you wanted to see him. How am I supposed to help you if you won't even let me see the man on which you dote?"

"H..Help me?" Nixi echoed a déjà vu of confusion.

"Well yeah, There are loopholes to our curse. For instance, if you scream his name and your admiration for him just under the surface, he will hear you, and never again will he leave the coast nor the ocean waters. He would not know why he had such an affinity for the sea, but he would spend the rest of his life not far from you." Benthesikyme stopped, lost in thought and then as if longing for someone. She let out a loud sigh.

"Of course, there is a downside. You have to watch them grow old and die without you. Knowing they wait for you, but to be any closer to them, they would die. I suppose there is a downside to every good thing in life." she shrugged, her voice starting to drift off as if Benthesikyme had been pulled off into a memory she could not escape. Nixi wondered if her sister was speaking from experience. Her actions seemed to imply that she had watched her love grow old and die, never knowing her. Nixi didn't want that kind of love. She wanted to be with him. She wanted to spend the rest of her life beside him.

She swam toward the bridge, unsure if she would get to see Dorus. Part of her wanted him not to appear so that she could keep him to herself. Her sister had not instilled in her trust when it came to Benthesikyme seeing him. Both to her joy and fear, she saw the blonde man sitting on the fishing pier next to the bridge. His feet were hanging off the side, and she thought she could touch him if she just reached out. Nixi's thoughts were heavy, and the reality of her love was coming to light for the first time. She could hold him close for a minute until he drowned or let him live his life out and never know what it was like for her lips to touch his. She wouldn't know what spending days and late nights with him would be like. She could spare her happiness for him or have a moment of romance in exchange for his life.

There was no in-between. No grey area to make her love work.

She peered out of the water, hiding under the pier where he sat. His feet brushed the water. She stared at his shadow stretched across the water and quietly cried, knowing that this moment would be the closest she would ever get to being with him. She was condemned never to have him in her life. Suddenly her life did not seem worth living. She swam hard and fast away from the harbor back home. Unable to escape her tears fast enough. Benthesikyme followed her after her abrupt departure. They returned home in silence. Nixi went straight to her room. It would be days before anyone saw her.

Chapter 7: The Sea Witch

Her sisters took turns checking in on Nixi while she sulked. All of them had questioned as to what ailed her, and she'd simply reply,

"I'm fine." She had never been an angsty type, so it was met with great concern. When her sisters brought food, she ate it but did not go to the banquet hall herself. After three days, she packed a handful of her things and returned to the harbor. There was a new air about the town. A somber hold on what once felt so joyous. She would never get to be with him, but if she was patient enough, she might be able to see him. After a day or two, she would return to the palace for a week, and with each visit, she would return in a better mood. After a day or two, she would return to the angsty version of herself. He may never know of her existence, but she could at least love him from afar. When she would see him, her heart leapt with joy, but upon her return home, the pleasure would quickly diminish as she reflected on their destiny and once more mourned the loss of her love.

She couldn't escape the woes of their future, knowing that he had become too valuable to her to make him sacrifice himself for her love, whether by life or obsession. She would equally watch the man who had heard her. His name was Tiberius, and he had the love of a woman and their child. At one time, he was a loving and attentive member of his family and community, but when he heard her voice, his caring nature was replaced with obsession. He no longer had moments alone because if left unattended, he would jump into the river to find a woman that barely existed. Many people kept an eye on him, and Nixi knew that he was loved. He, however, disregarded it all for a voice that she swore would never again cross his ears. She watched Dorus as a reminder of the fate of her love if she ever broke her silence. Upon her return, one of her sisters would check in on her, and though they all knew about her lovesickness, it was Despoine that commiserated with her the best. Nixi would spend hours talking about her visit to his town and the subsequent heartache that came with it. Occasionally, Despoine would counsel her other sisters about any notable changes that may have happened over the visit.

One day Kymopoleia barged into Nixi's room, startling Nixi to the point that she visibly jumped.

"You startled me!" she exclaimed. She managed a half smile before her eyes dropped back to the wall she had been blankly staring at.

"Good," Kymopoleia stated. "I can confidently say that I am over your pity party. It has been well over a month of your distance from your friends and family, and we miss you too much! So you know what you have to do?" Nixi shook her head no as she guessed,

"Leave my room?" Kymopoleia nodded.

"Life has become too dull without you, so you must leave your room. I'm not saying you need to return to the banquet hall or join us for the tales told. So let's just start with something simple. Let's you, me and Benthesikyme go for a swim! There is something we want to show you. It's a secret, so you can tell no one. Do you want to learn a secret?" Kymopoleia asked. Nixi loved mysteries and knew that her sister would not tolerate no as an answer. The secret was only a lure to fish her out of the room. She had no choice but to accept, but her heart sparked in a quiet joy at the prospect of learning a secret.

Nixi was several miles from her room when Benthesikyme and Kymopoleia mentioned that the mystery was a ruse to make her leave. As she began to whine in protest of such a long swim, she realized she did not recognize the area they were in. With alarm in her voice, she recommended they return home, but with that suggestion, Kymopoleia grabbed her wrist, pulling her deeper into unknown waters. They squeezed through a reef that had not been used much and was bordering on a ruin of the sea. Benthesikyme went first as Nixi followed. Kymopoleia took up the rear sandwiching Nixi between them so that escape would be more challenging. It was exhilarating and terrifying when she broke past the reef ruins into the barren land ahead of her. Nixi thought this must be what Benthesikyme and Kymopoleia aimed to show her. A new place to explore, and as she became comfortable with this exploration, she was surprised that Kymopoleia grabbed her wrist and continued further into the barely occupied waters. The pace at which her sisters swam quickened, and Nixi struggled to keep up.

Nixi began to realize they were in the same barren lands that her grandmother, Amphitrite, would tell the most terrifying tales about. For Nixi, this land had an ominous aura about it. She imagined the stories from this land, and her scales crawled as she hesitated to follow her sister any farther. It was unacceptable in Kymopoleia's opinion to turn back, so once more, she grabbed Nixi and pulled her further into deeper waters.

As they progressed, deeper Nixi's fear was replaced with thrill and possible madness as she sped up, and her sister abandoned her grip on Nixi. Nixi got lost in the enjoyment of doing something she knew was wrong. It was filled with so much potential for terrible outcomes that, for the first time since her introduction to Dorus, she was able to escape the sadness brought on by the thoughts of her love. She dived further down into the darkness that stretched beneath. She swam as fast as she could into the abyss, wondering how deep she could go before fear or pressure sickness forced her to pack up.

Kymopoleia's voice tore through her thoughts, and Nixi abruptly stopped as if she was attached to a chain anchored by her sister, snapping her back into reality. Nixi returned enthusiastically to her sister's side.

"Thank you for taking me here. This is the best I've felt in what feels like an eternity" Kymopoleia turned to Nixi, her eyes darker than usual.

"We aren't here for fun and games. This area is just as terrible as the stories Amphtrite has told you about." Nixi's eyes became wide as she was filled with a haunting caution. Why would her sisters take her to such a place that could jeopardize one, if not all, of them?

"I have to ask you a question." Kymopoleia's voice broke through the darkness with a tone that made Nixi shiver from the discomfort. "I need you to answer it honestly. A level of honesty you might not have recognized until now." Nixi was now terrified. An honesty that she might not even have with herself? She had never seen her sister so serious. The unfamiliar somber tune of Kymopoleia and the haunting location shook her with an apprehension she had not been familiar with. She wondered what would be so important that her sisters would put them both at such significant risk. Each thought Nixi had to answer her question grew evermore terrifying, and she was consumed by apprehension.

"When Benthesikyme told you that you could bind the guy you have been pining over to you, why did you not do it?" Nixi was blind-sighted. What did her actions, or lack thereof, have to do with being in such a terrifying part of the sea?

"You were given a way to keep your love close to you and not risk his death, but you didn't take it. Why?" Kymopoleia said quizzically. Nixi stumbled over words as the sorrow once again filled her. What a cruel joke her sisters had put her through, distracting her from her sadness only to abruptly rip it open with such force and ferocity.

"I have seen what has happened to the man who heard my voice. I've seen the destruction that it has caused to him and everyone around him. He may be with them in body, but he is always looking for me in spirit. I…" Nixi stammered. "I just couldn't stand knowing that he would be attached to me against his will. I'd rather lose him and think of him having a happy life than be forced to stay for a reason he will never understand!" She began to sob as though letting the truth out had released some of her burdens. It had also released emotions she had been holding back since she realized her fate was to leave him be. Kymopoleia's eyes softened. "I was worried that was your answer."

Nixi was confused. Why did they drag her out to the middle of nowhere and to such an ominous place to ask her treacherous questions? Kymopoleia sighed. Benthesikyme swam forward.

"We promised you a secret, and here is one that no one else knows, and I rather they didn't. I was once in love with a human." Nixi immediately gave all her attention to her Benthesikyme. She would have never expected to learn of such a thing from her. She was, after all, the most averse to humans and spent most of her time immersed in the affairs of the sea. "I was greedy and called out to her, and she waited for me." she continued.

"That wasn't enough. I tried to find a loophole, a way for us to be together indefinitely. Eventually, Amphitrite discovered my love, and she flipped. She likes humans less than I do, as you are well aware. She demanded that I call her to my side. Where my love would surely meet her demise. I refused, and when I returned to gaze upon her, I found her tied to an anchor at the bottom of the sea." Benthesikyme choked. "She had done to her what I refused to do and left her there for me to find. I would give anything to have not decided to call out to her. To never have loved her." She began to cry, and as her tears hit the floor, sand dollars appeared with each tear. Nixi realized for the first time that the sand dollars she had seen throughout the palace were her sister's tears. A constant reminder of her love and her loss. Likely as a reminder of the dangers that come from meddling with humans.

"Amphitrite once told me that if I ever spoke on the matter, my tears would not be the only reminder of my loss." Nixi embraced her sister.

"I am so sorry!" Nixi thought about her sister carrying the fate of her lover's death for so long. She didn't know how long ago the tryst was, but any amount of time quietly grieving was too much heartache to have. Nixi was conflicted in a shared grief at her sister's loss and her own torn fate. She became angry that Amphitrite, their grandmother, would do such terrible things to her sister. "I didn't know," Nixi said softly. Kymopoleia shook Nixi off her as Benthesikyme quickly dried her eyes.

"No one is supposed to know. Amphitrite would do terrible things if she knew we were here. That I told you about her and for what I'm about to tell you." Her face turned into a scowl showing her teeth that reminded Nixi of a dragonfish she once saw in the banquet hall. It had been put out there as a tribute. She recalled that the person who had captured and given them the dragonfish said they lived in these depths.

"I resent that woman with every fiber of my being," she growled. Nixi didn't know what to say. What could she say? How could she console someone who had lived with such a heart-wrenching void? Just thinking about her sister's pain was too much to bear, and the fact that she had endured it alone without any hint of the scope of her loss, she realized how strong her sister was. She now realized that the dangers of her love were more detrimental than she could truly fathom.

"I'm so sorry, I never knew," she kept saying under her breath because she couldn't think of any other words to say.

Benthesikyme gained some distance between herself and Nixi as if trying to escape the memory once more. Kymopoleia turned to Nixi.

"You know about my history, so I won't bore you. We aren't here to relive the past. I think we'd all rather forget that we each even have one. We brought you here because even Amphitrite doesn't come out this far. There is something in these waters that I think even Amphitrite is afraid of." The fear once more returned to Nixi. Something her grandmother feared was sure to be terrible indeed. Her grandmother scared the ink out of her, and she could only dream of what monstrosities were in the waters that her sisters had taken her to.

Nixi spent her time trying to avoid her grandmother due to a fear of her, so she did not want to face a new bigger bad. "What's that?" Nixi quietly asked, desperately fearing the answer.

"I never stopped thinking about her," Kymopoleia said to herself.

"I have spent years trying to find a way to be with her. I even swam so deep that I rapped upon the door to Hades himself." her words drifted off, and Benthesikyme picked up the trail as if they were both telling the same story.

"Unfortunately, it is too late for us to be together, but we may be able to help you. In my quest to be reunited with my love, I encountered someone who could do many things that most could not. If you can pay the price, they may reunite you with your love." Nixi's heart fluttered at the idea that she could find her way to him.

"What is the cost? I'm not willing to sacrifice him if that is what you are thinking," Nixi declared sternly.

Kymopoleia looked at Nixi as if she was stupid, and though she said nothing, Nixi got the impression,

'Why would I tell you about my hardships only to make you have the same.' Nixi then felt stupid.

"Do you remember the folktale of the first mermaid? A goddess who loved a human but then killed him, so she was banished to the ocean depths?" Nixi nodded. She thought a lot about that story since she first learned of her curse on humans. She had decided that she hated the goddess for cursing her in the wake of her actions. She was, in Nixi's opinion, the reason why she could not be with the human she so desperately wanted to know. "Well, she is known to live in these waters and has cultivated great powers in her time in the sea. She is known here as a witch and may be as powerful as Amphitrite herself. So we figured we could find her and plead your case, and maybe she can unite you with the human you adore."

Nixi's preconception about the fallen goddess immediately conflicted with the new hope her sister had given her. Would the person who had been the cause of her affliction also be the cure? If she is, would she be willing to help? More importantly, what would be the price, and could Nixi pay it so that she would be united with the human she held so dear? She resolved that she would find the infamous sea witch and find out more. She knew if she returned home, she would always wonder, and Nixi felt that she owed it to her sisters, who both could not proceed to find her way to her love to pursue the ending with her human that they could not have. She nodded at Kymopoleia, and her sister broke into a smile. They began to swim around the deep waters asking what few animals they crossed about where they might find the sea witch. After some time, they found themselves in front of a cave. Benthesikyme and Kymopoleia nudged her forward. Benthesikyme notified Nixi that they would wait for her at the cave's mouth because going in would surely awaken their memories and, with it, the feelings of loss, which they were sure would result in each of them wishing for death. So Nixi cautiously entered the cave.

"He… Hello?" she called out to no answer as her sister gestured her to go further in until she could see her sister no more.

Chapter 8: Reunited

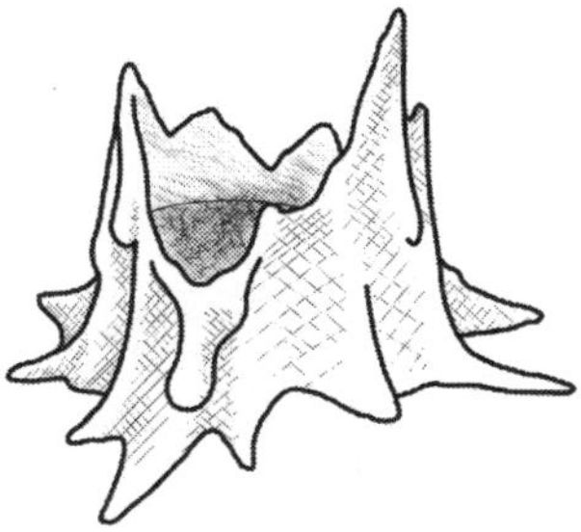

Atargatis waited in darkness for Amphitrite to return with her child. Time slipped by, and Amphitrite never came. Even Poseidon had left her to her own devices. She was allowed to go, but she found she couldn't. She feared that her daughter would return to her, and when that moment came, she wanted to be as easy to find as possible. She would occasionally leave the cave she now called home for food and other mundane tasks. She could not return to the beaches of her past because it would remind her of love and loss simultaneously. She could not look for her daughter because she feared it would endanger her dear child. She resolved to see her daughter again and would do everything possible to make that happen. She was not completely helpless in the prison that she found herself confined to. She was a goddess, and though her domain was that of the tide and fertility, she knew she was capable of many things. It was time for her to adapt.

When she first began to leave the confines of her cave, she would not venture far, but with time her invisible chain binding her to her home would extend. She first began to harness her power with tactics she was familiar with. First, by helping a megachasma pelagios couple get pregnant. With their child's birth, many of the creatures that resided in those deep waters found their way to her cave to seek help in fertility. She found ease in the adaptation of fertility, from humans to ocean creatures, and soon it was not just sea creatures looking to breed but also lonely lovers looking to find their mate. Her powers began to adapt easier, and she knew that although she enjoyed helping those that came to her, she had a mission to reunite with her only love left. She would find a way to see her daughter once more. It was in that quest that she found herself at Hades' door. Hades was a lonely but passionate man. He had heard of a witch near his oceanic hell mouth that could facilitate finding a partnership, so he sent some messengers to retrieve her for a meeting.

Atargatis was timid of Hades. He was the brother of the man who had assaulted her for so many years, and so when he called for her, she was crippled with fear. She feared that he, too, would brutalize her but also feared that rejecting him would make her life worse. So she gathered herself and swallowed her fear, answering his call. When she entered his domicile, she transformed into the woman she once was. Her old body felt foreign and uncomfortable. She saw a reflecting pool in the middle of the room and, with some hesitation, peered into it. It did not reflect her image; instead, she saw Adad's face and cried out. It had been so long that she had thought she would have forgotten his face, but she had remembered every smile line and hair follicle he had. The image changed to a young child. The child had eyes that reminded her of Adad, and although the child looked human from the waist up, below her waist was a tail with scales that shone. The child's laughter ignited joy in her heart, and she knew it was her child, Samiramis. She gasped as tears of joy began to creep across her face. It brought her so much comfort, but in the reflection, the child was called Nixi. The child bounced with joy into the arms of another young mermaid, and a wave of relief swept over Atargatis. Her daughter was alive, happy, and thriving. She could not ask for more peace of mind.

When Hades entered the room, she looked up briefly from the pool, and when she looked back down, there was nothing but her own reflection. Her heart sank. She sat with Hades, and he told her of his woes in companionship. He was desperate to spend his life and death with someone. She had often heard the plea for love, and finding partners for the lonely was a pleasure.

When Hades had finished talking about his desperation for love, Atargatis once more approached the pool that had shown her her most beloved person and stuck her finger in it. The ripples from the intrusion morphed into a young woman's face. She called the god over to the pool, and he looked at the woman in the reflection. Hades gasped at the sight of her. She was beautiful and held a warmth that he had so rarely seen. Atargatis removed her finger, and the image disappeared. "Find that woman and bring her here. When you do, send this melanocetus johnsonii to retrieve me." She gestured toward the entrance she arrived in, and a fish emerged from the darkness.

"I will facilitate your bonding. Now, let us talk about payment." Hades' fingers entwined each other.

"I have heard that I have the man you love in my possession, and with the uniting of love for me, I will do the same for you." Atargatis' heart clenched. She could be with her lover once more. Her heart leapt into her throat, and she choked on the emotion before swallowing it again.

"No, I require that as payment." she confidently pointed at the pool that gave her a moment of joy by showing her Samiramis. She knew she might never get to meet her daughter, but with that pool, she could, at the very least, watch her from afar. Hades looked at the reflecting pool. That mirror was his only connection away from that of the underworld, and in giving it to her, he would not be able to see a world apart from his own. He would, however, be exchanging it for a wife, and in obtaining her, he would not need the pool, so with caution, he agreed to the payment but would only make the payment once the two had been married.

Atargatis returned home and began to plan for Hades' wedding day. Clearing a place for the basin, she was confident that she would obtain. It was a few months before the melanocetus johnsonii retrieved her. The cave bubbled with excitement and laughter as Atargatis' enthusiasm took hold. She could not recall a day she had found such high spirits, so she hurriedly returned to the hell mouth. Hades was quick to greet her though his face was sour. In exasperation, he spoke to Atargatis about the woman's disdain for him.

"How can I not be lonely if she is so cold? She does not have the warm smile she did when you showed her to me. She doesn't smile at all!" Atargatis soothed him and offered to speak on his behalf to her. The woman, Persephone, was escorted into the room that Hades and Atargatis had their first encounter, and with great hesitation and exacerbation, he left the two women alone.

Persephone ran to Atargatis, and as soon as they were alone, with tears in her eyes, she said,

"You have to help me! I have been imprisoned!" Atargatis felt pain all too familiar to her.

"Calm, child," she cooed. "What terrible misfortune has befallen you?" She led her to a chair and sat her down. The girl then told her the tale of what had transpired. Her father, Zeus, had promised her to Hades to wed. Upon that agreement, she was sent to the underworld and into isolation. She did not get to say goodbye to her friends, life, or mother. She was able to explore the entire kingdom Hades ruled, but that was not enough for her.

"If I could speak to my mother, I would at least have someone." Atargatis put an arm around the distraught woman and led her to the pool that had shown Hades the visage of Persephone on her last visit. She pulled a thread from it.

"This is your thread of fate. This thread has shown me here is where you are destined to be. The wife to Hades. In this thread, there is love in its purest form. His love for you and, in time, your love for him. I know that love feels improbable currently, but I assure you this match has great potential. It only requires your patience." Persephone eyes filled with tears.

"There is nothing but loneliness and loss here. I can not love someone who would bring me such an ill fate. I won't!" she exclaimed. Atargatis put the thread back into the pool.

"Would you let me talk to him on your behalf? See if I can come to an amicable solution?" Persephone nodded to the request. She could not control her fate, but this woman may be able to ensure her freedom.

Atargatis excused herself from the room and entered Hades' throne room. He sat next to a vacant throne obviously made for his queen.

"She hates me!" he pouted. "I had loneliness, but now it's filled with disdain. I wanted a partner, a wife! You have given me nothing but contempt!" Atargatis spoke directly.

"You have not cultivated a wife! You have cultivated a prisoner! Her disdain is your doing, not mine!" Hades' temperament flared. Who was this creature so unabashed in her address to him? "You want to fend off loneliness but have only spread it!" His heart pained, knowing that although he would never admit to this woman's words, there may be a bit of truth to the statement. His temper cooled.

"What am I to do?" he sadly muttered. Atargatis approached him and took his hand.

"You give her that which you yourself cannot have." She materialized a pomegranate and placed it in the hand she held of his. On your wedding day, give her this. It will allow her to leave the underworld for small stretches of time. In doing so, she can have everything she feels she has lost. She will be able to see her friends and family, and it'll let her return to you.

"You don't want a prisoner anymore than she wants to be one, I assure you." Hades slumped his shoulders as if his whole body had collapsed at the thought.

"What if I miss her too much? I want her by my side. Always."

"Letting yourself miss her will make your time together much more valuable, don't you think?" He bowed his head but did not disagree. Atargatis let go of his hand that now held the round fruit, and he pulled it closer to him. She excused herself, but before her exit, she recommended that he make Persephone a new-looking pool. One to rival her beauty so that she could see her world when she was in the underworld, and he could see her when she was not. He agreed, and she returned to Persophone.

"I have brokered a deal. You will spend 6 months a year with Hades; the other 6 will be yours to do as you, please. This will be in effect as long as his love for you is true. I know half a lunar cycle can feel like an eternity when you feel like a prisoner, but I implore you to try to find something to love in that god. With your love and care, I know he can become the man you've always dreamt of being with and the god he is destined to become. Your fates are intertwined." Persephone sighed in relief and pulled Atargatis into her arms. It had been so long since she had felt an embrace that it startled her and felt unnatural. Atargatis did not want to reject the affection she had become so unaccustomed to but did nothing to reciprocate it. When Persophone released her grasp Hades walked into the room, and she smiled at him. It was the first flicker of warmth Hades had ever felt, and he vowed to himself he would do anything to feel the warmth of his bride. No matter the cost. He then gestured to some guards who approached the pool and began to move it to any location of Atargatis' desire.

Once the pool was appropriately placed in her cave, the guards returned to the underworld, and Atargatis peered into it. Once more, images of Semiramis came to the surface. She took comfort in being able to be so close to her. She now had the opportunity to see her daughter, who others called Nixi, grow up. She began adapting her powers into more impressive modifications until she was renowned for her mystical powers. She found joy in helping others heal from whatever ailed them. When able, she occasionally sent messengers to deliver gifts she knew Nixi liked to the castle. There were never any notes left for the present, and sometimes another would grab the treat before Nixi could receive it, but when she did, Atargatis would smile for days. A ripple effect from Nixi's own smile. Before Atargatis knew it, over a century had passed.

She saw Nixi turn 180. She watched Nixi have her first taste of a barnacle and how her whole body lit up joyfully. She saw her call out to a man and the repercussions of such an event. She watched as her daughter spent days alone, wrestling between her heart and logic, and desperately wished she could help. She was able to help so many creatures that had found themselves at her doorstep, but Nixi was so far away. She knew that distance would be their fate. There were days the heartache was unbearable, and she could not bear to look in the reflection pool. On other days she ached to see her daughter and could not pull herself away from her image.

On this day, Atargatis found comfort in the darkness. Dreaming of all the dreams she once had, sitting in the dark, hoping for a day different from the cycle she had committed to. She had made a name for herself over time, and a desperate creature would periodically find its way to her. After her merger between Hades and Persephone had been a success, many came to her looking for love, fertility, and on occasion, malice. She would do what she could to ease the ache that those that found her all had. The cave now contained a myriad of potions and ingredients to help facilitate whatever problems crossed her door, and she had made a small fortune in doing so.

Her needs were little, but she had enough to give her as much comfort as she desired. She desired little, so often, her payment requests were arbitrary. An eye of a llama was requested of a sturgeon who had lost their eggs and needed to know if any of their offspring had survived. Atargatis would reunite a mother with some of her surviving children upon payment. Humans had gathered the rest and eaten them. The tears of a broken heart had been a payment from one of Nixi's cohabitants that she identified as a sister. The cost of mermaid tears was given in exchange for removing a name from her heart. When Atargatis took the name from the young girl's heart, she left the love there. The young girl, named Kymopoleia, didn't want to forget her in fear of making the mistake of loving a human again but knew that talking of her love would end in a fate much worse than the feeling of loss. So the girl endured the sadness but could not place a name on the human she had once loved so deeply.

"He...Hello?" A voice emerged from the darkness. Atargatis pulled herself up and made herself somewhat presentable. She had a client! She quickly tidied the area and then got into her persona of the sea witch she carried so well.

"Yes, my child, come closer.." She announced into the darkness. She heard the visitor hesitate and added, "I am a busy creature. I do not have all day. Either come here or go away!" A figure was now visible in the archway to Atargatis' casting area. It approached cautiously, and so Atargatis cast an illumination to the room. The room became dimly lit. Atargatis did not enjoy bright light. That was a version of her that had long died. As the room brightened, the visitor could see more than the darkness. Not accustomed to such dim light, the new client still struggled with sight, having complete darkness replaced by long shadows. They swam toward the light and soon were in the same cavern as Atargatis.

"I was told you might be able to help me unite with someone?" the girl called out. Atargatis was paralyzed. She could not believe that before her was her daughter Samiramis, who knew themselves to be Nixi. Atargatis wanted to run to her and give her all the love she had been holding inside for as long as they had been apart. She could not. Nixi knew nothing about her. She knew that Nixi, as did everyone else, thought she had been the result of Amphitrite's discretion. It would be unfair to Nixi for Atargatis to unload such a vibrant history that the two shared. She gestured for Nixi to take a seat, and Nixi diligently obeyed. It was evident to Atargatis that Nixi was scared of her.

"What brings you to my door?" Atargatis said as coolly as possible.

"My sisters, Benthesikyme and Kymopoleia, told me you could help me?" She looked at the ground, afraid to make eye contact with the sea witch.

"Help you reunite with what?" "Oh," Nixi hesitated.

"There is this human that I want to be with desperately. I love him, but our destiny is torn because we are from two worlds. I want to… uh.. Stop that?" Her voice ended on a high note. Atargatis swam to her and grabbed her hands. Nixi froze, obviously too afraid to move and suffer wrath. Atargatis looked down, pretending to study Nixi's hands before letting them go.

"There is little to be done about the chasm that splits the human world from the world of gods," Atargatis said flatly. Nixi's head hung in disappointment, and Atargatis wanted to throw her arms around her and promise that she would do anything to unite her to her love. She knew all would suffer if Amphitrite learned about such a union. She could handle her suffering, and the man's suffering had no meaning to her, but to watch Nixi suffer at the hands of Amphitrite, she knew she could not handle it. Nixi got up and quietly approached the door.

Atargatis didn't want her to go. She desired to lock them into this moment so that she could spend the rest of eternity in the company of her daughter.

"Wait!" she pleaded. "There may be no way to merge the two worlds, but what if you became of one world?" Nixi stopped and returned to the side of Atargatis, awaiting her to go on.

"I can turn you into a human. If I do, you will have to sever ties with everything you know your life to be. All family, friends, everything you love about your life and many things you don't. You would lose it all. In exchange, you will become human and be one with him in the land of people."

Nixi perked up with lively interest. "You need to take a month to think about if you are sincerely okay with giving up all you know for something so unknown. Do not discuss this offer with anyone, or the agreement will be canceled. If, in a month of quiet reflection, you think this is the path for you, return here, and we shall proceed." Nixi bounced up with a beaming smile.

"Thank you! I can't wait to see you in a month!" She made her way to the door with quick enthusiasm.

"Do not take this offer lightly," Atargatis warned. "Giving up everything is no easy task." Nixi nodded. "Before you go, we have to talk about payment."

Atargatis's voice trailed off as she moved into the darkness.

"What would that be." Nixi's voice filled with great concern. She thought about how many treasures would be asked of her and wondered if she could even get the payment.

Atargatis had dreamt of this scenario as she watched Nixi pine over the human. If given the opportunity, how would she be able to help her daughter without suffering the plausible wrath of Amphitrite? If she could get Nixi out of the water, then Amphitrite would have no hold on either Nixi or herself. Another fact she had mulled over was Nixi's sirens call. No matter what Nixi's form became, her voice would always be a gateway to obsession and madness. A curse brought onto her by Poseidons obsession and her mother's madness. So she would need to remove Nixi's voice. It would be the only way to contain the curse she was afflicted with. She hadn't figured it all out but knew she would figure out the solution. She needed to. She wanted to do something for her daughter. She wanted to contribute to her happiness even though she knew she could never be a part of it.

"The payment will be your voice," Atargatis said dryly.

"My voice?" Nixi snapped back.

"Yes. I told you this transaction would cost you everything. That is a part of everything." Nixi hesitated.

The cost made her question if becoming human would be worth the sacrifice. She now understood the severity of the exchange. Would she be willing to be so alone for one person to whom she had never actually talked to? When Nixi emerged from the cave, Benthesikyme and Kymopoleia enthusiastically rushed her.

"What did the witch say?" they said in unison. Nixi shook her head.

"She said there wasn't a way to get what I want." She hoped that saying that wouldn't breach their contract. She had one month to keep a secret and make a life-altering decision. They swam back in silence. Benthesikyme and Kymopoleia assumed it was because of the rejection and tried to console her sister.

"I'm sorry she couldn't do anything. Maybe we can find another witch?" Kymopoleia piped. Nixi raised her head with a hopeful look on her face.

"Do you know of another sea witch?" Now it was Kymopoleia that hung her head in dismay. "No," both Benthesikyme and Kymopoleia she said softly. They returned home quietly, and Nixi returned to sulking in her room for a few days before returning to the harbor to watch Dorus. Would he be worth the sacrifice to let them be together? She had only a month to decide.

Chapter 9: Enchanted

Her sisters took turns checking in on Nixi, bringing little gifts. Small bribes to get her sister to return from her depression. Nixi tried to play it cool and join them in whatever trivial adventures they came up with, but she didn't enjoy it much. She would fake pleasantries and feign enjoyment so her friends and family wouldn't worry. She also tried to appreciate her moments with them, knowing that this might be the last time she did anything with those she cared about most. Nixi knew, in her heart, she would likely sacrifice everything and become human just to find out if Dorus was everything she hoped he would be. If she didn't take this opportunity, she would spend the rest of her life wondering if she had made the right choice. If she turned and things didn't work out, she would at least know it was for the pursuit of love.

Each day that passed became a bit sweeter as she became more comfortable leaving her home in pursuit of love. She made sure to make every moment memorable with her family because she knew the life she had known would miss her and wanted to remember every moment so she would never feel like she was gone forever. She spent one week at the harbor watching Dorus go about his day. He seemed like a warm and caring man. She loved his laughter, and even his moments looking at the sea left a desire to be by his side, looking out into the water with him.

One day in particular, Dorus was sitting on the pier with his feet in the water, fishing. She hid under the dock, encased in the shadows. She was so elated to be so close to him that she couldn't help herself and lightly touched his foot. He immediately yelped in surprise, pulling his feet from the water. He then chuckled to himself for being so startled by a fish swimming by, and he plunked his feet back into the water.

"Get a hold of yourself, man!" He shook his head, chuckling. "Well, I at least know the fish are around. They just need to take the bait." He pulled his rod up to see there was no longer bait on it, so he wrapped a tiny bit of meat on the gorge and cast it out once more. Nixi had observed a fish steal the bait and wanted to know what the strange meat tasted like. So after a few minutes, she gently unwrapped the gorge and took a nibble. The meat was chewy and tasted unnatural. Would this be the food she would have to eat? Would there be no more barnacles in her future? The thought of giving up her favorite food hurt more than the idea of leaving her family behind.

'If humans didn't eat sea creatures, why would they be so intent on capturing fish?' She thought as she recalled Triton cutting up a net and freeing the fish on one of his swims; she tagged along on. She felt ease sweep over her. She could still eat some of what she was accustomed to. Dorus started singing a little tune,

"Come little fishies to my call, take my bait and make my belly full" Nixi was astonished. It was like he had read her mind. They would eat creatures of the sea, and he was singing for her to come to him. When he left, having caught nothing because Nixi kept eating the bait and warding fish off, Nixi quickly headed home. She knew that he was where she needed to be. So she set out to say subtle goodbyes to her family and return to the sea witch. She was ready to make any sacrifice to be with the man she knew she was sure to love.

She was timid upon her return to the witch. The vacant land surrounding her had an ominous feel, exacerbated by her solitude. When she saw a creature, she asked for directions to ensure she was going the right way. Everyone knew who she was, and they had pleasant things to say about the witch, but Nixi still felt nervous about turning to this creature for her romantic salvation. When Nixi made it to the cave, she swam as confidently as possible despite fearing a myriad of what-if scenarios. When she entered the sea witch's cavern, she saw the witch with a couple of squids. She was casting a fertility enchantment, and both squids garbled with glee when they were handed a talisman and a set of instructions. When done, they swam past, eyes bright with encouragement to both themselves and, for whatever reason, the merchild that had found their way to the witch.

Atargatis was thrilled when she looked up from her casting pool to see Nixi hovering around the doorway. She had been keeping a careful eye on Nixi's movements over the last month as she worked on making a spell that would turn her beloved daughter into a human and make it easier for people to understand her without having a voice. If her daughter had to become mute to get what she wanted, she wanted it to be easier to communicate with a look or body language. She wanted her daughter to succeed. She had been proud of Nixi for taking the matter so seriously. She had watched her give quiet goodbyes to those she knew and loved. As well as revisit the man to ensure she felt the transaction would be worth it.

Atargatis waved for Nixi to come into the room. Nixi approached and sat next to the pool where Atargatis had stared for countless hours, watching her daughter grow into the woman before her. Atargatis touched the liquid within the basin, and as she lifted her finger, Nixi could see the reflection of Dorus. He was smiling while talking to someone in the square where she had first seen him. During the day, it was a market, and by evening it was often a place of celebration. Nixi was so excited about all the things she would be able to do with him. In a wondrous world that she only knew tales of. Atargatis smiled as she watched Nixi stare into the pool. She pretended to rummage through her cabinets to look for the needed ingredients. In truth, she had already set them aside. The rummaging was just to prolong the time she could spend with Nixi. She knew this would likely be the last time she'd be around her daughter, so she wanted to milk it for every moment she could get with the child.

Atargatis made a meal for them to share. Nixi expressed an urgency to get the spell done, but Atargatis said, "It takes a lot of energy for a spell of this magnitude. So I need to eat. You should join me, as this spell will have an equal toll on you." Though it was a truthful statement, Atargatis mostly wanted to have every moment available with her unknowing daughter.

Once they had finished their meal, Atargatis began to brew the potions. There were three that needed to be made. One to turn her into a human, one to silence her and lock her voice in a shell she had acquired, and the final to make her language out of silence easier for people to understand. She could have had two of the potions already made, as only the changing form one required blood magic. Atargatis decided to do them all on the spot to impress her child with how much she was willing to do for Nixi. Nixi took the voice and body language potions on site. Shooting them back like shots. The awful taste grew bolder in its disgust before settling down on Nixi's pallet. Atargatis gathered some travel items. They had to go to the harbor for the final potion because it was unlikely she would know how to swim after she transformed.

It was late evening when they arrived in the quiet, sleepy city before them. Nixi had led Atargatis to the bridge where she had first seen Dorus. It was a unique spot for Nixi and had become a pivotal place in her heart. Atargatis pulled out a bottle and gestured for Nixi to lay out her hand. She immediately cut into Nixi's finger, and Nixi yelped in a silent hurt surprise. Atargatis said nothing. Instead, she immediately placed Nixi's finger over the bottle. The blood filled the bottle's rim, and when her blood reached the concoction, she could feel her finger tingle.

When Atargatis pulled Nixi's finger off the bottle opening, she saw that the fluid was gone. The spell had seeped into the cut, and she had absorbed it. A mere minute after the spell had entered her bloodstream, Nixi was confronted with an extreme pain that made her feel like she was turning inside out. She began to choke, gasping at water and air, undecided which one she needed. Atargatis put an air bubble to encapsulate Nixi's head. Air rushed into her lungs as she spat out the salty sea that she had already breathed in. Soon Nixi was flailing, trying to figure out what to do with the silly legs that had replaced her tail. Once the transformation was complete, Atargatis flung her onto the banks that the bridge spread between. Nixi rolled over, gasping for air, trying to control the pain of being torn apart.

Atargatis placed some clothes beside her, whispering for her to put them on. Nixi had no idea how to put on clothes, so she tried draping them over her, and Atargatis shook her head no. She mimed how the clothes were supposed to go on. Mimicking, sticking her head into the head hole and then her arms in their respective spots. When Nixi finally had the shirt on in such a way that the sea witch approved, she was handed a skirt which Nixi put her head through. Now familiar with head holes, she stuck her head in, thinking about how big this head hole was compared to the last. Atargatis told her to shimmy it down until it met her waist and tighten the skirt so it would not fall. Atargatis pulled away and smiled. "I think you are ready to go!" With the sea witch cheering her on, she got on her feet and clumsily stumbled until she fell back to the ground. Nixi tried again and could walk a little farther before the ground dragged her back down.

An hour went by before Nixi really understood how to master walking, and it was then that Atargatis took her leave. She didn't want to go. She wanted to join her daughter and tell her everything. Atargatis let out a long sigh as she returned back home. This had been the best day that Atargatis had ever had. She didn't tell Nixi she was her mother, even though she wanted the world to know that Nixi was her child. She thought about trying to join her, but even in the shade of darkness, the world above the sea was too bright for her to be able to stay. She was not the woman she used to be. That pleasure of when she walked the line between man and sea was rotting in her past. She was no longer that fulfilled spirit that held the man she loved so close. Now Atatgatis was destined to live in the home she made at the bottom of the ocean. She could still see Nixi in the pool, and once more, she returned to a life of a quiet spectator.

Nixi fell asleep under the bridge as soon as Atargatis left. She could not recall a time when she was so exhausted. Every cell in her body ached. She had never known such pain to exist. She had thought she would turn human and meet Dorus the same night but could not pull herself out from under the bridge. She awoke on the banks under the bridge when she heard some children laughing. She stumbled out from the bridge, and the bright sunlight hit her skin like the lapping flicker of flame. She squinted as she shuffled herself up to the road. A carriage trotted by her, and she was enamored with the magical beast that pulled it. She began to follow it and found herself at the town square.

There was so much to look at. Things shone and glittered, tapestries of delicate beauty and smells that filled the whole square, crashing into each other, creating a beautiful melody in her nasal cavity. She found herself overwhelmed and tried to exit to gasp for less pungent air. When she saw a vendor that sold fresh fish, she tried to grab one, but the vendor stopped her. "That's one hemiobol young lady!" Nixi removed her hand. She wasn't sure what the vendor was talking about, but she got the impression that she was not allowed to have the fish. She left the square and returned to the familiar terrain of the bridge.

Nixi felt she might have made a drastic error when choosing land. She was alone and had no understanding of the human world. How could she have been so ill-prepared? She stood on the bridge where Dorus had stood with his friend long ago. She looked out at the water, trying to hold back the tears she knew were building with each new and overwhelming experience. She choked back tears she refused to shed. A chronic ache from her eyes as they began to fill with water.

"It's beautiful out there, isn't it," a man said from behind her. She nodded and brushed the tears off her eyelids and into her top. The man walked up beside her.

"I understand that. I feel a calling every time I look out into the water." The man smiled at her to reassure her that she would be okay.

"There was a time when I'd look out at sea and see a vast emptiness. One day I felt the waters call to me, and I realized that despite the vast emptiness I saw beneath the waters, there was a world I could hardly imagine, but I wanted to see with every ounce of my being. Some people saw my devotion to what I could not see as madness." The man smiled.

"I guess it was, but I didn't mind it. However, when I saw you, I felt a peace I hadn't felt in an eternity. Maybe we share a madness?" The man turned to face the young woman. Nixi immediately recognized Tiberius, the man who had heard her voice. Even out of the water, she could tell that something in him could recognize her.

"What's your name, young lady?" Nixi opened her mouth to speak, but no noise came from it. Her cheeks flushed, and her head bowed.

"Not much for words then, are you?" Tiberius chuckled. He was a much older man than she had realized. Shades of grey covered his temples, and his eyes had wrinkles around the edges. His smile was warm and comforting. Nixi shook her head in agreement with not being a person of many or any words.

Tiberius had seen the woman at the bridge, and his heart rocketed upward. He got the same satisfaction looking at her as when jumping in the river, trying to find a feeling that was always a little further ahead. Tiberius had at one point not been allowed to go near the water alone, for his family feared his drowning himself because of the madness the ocean waters had cast on him. It wasn't him that really suffered the siren call, as he was more than happy to follow it to unknown depths. He had finally adjusted to the desire of the ocean's calling but did not act on it because he had a wife and child he cherished. It was for them that he stopped jumping into the river to find a voice that was indeed only in his head. Then he saw her, and all his desire for the sea seemed to fixate on the young girl.

"Are you hungry?" Nixi nodded her head. "Come over to our house. We would very much appreciate you joining us for dinner tonight." Nixi bowed in agreement, and Tiberius escorted her to his family's domicile. His wife was elated when she saw the girl at her doorstep. The girl was fair with long wavy hair. She had an unspoken beauty that equaled her silence. Both his wife and daughter fawned over her. She was someone in need, and they were happy to try and fill the void. For the first time in months, Tiberius had engaged with his family, so they took her in. With her around, his family felt the presence of a husband and father that had been slipping away.

His daughter, Sophia, brushed her hair, and his wife, Agda, found a garment they could give her. She was a beauty to behold, even in their rags, and the whole family embraced her. She had learned a lot from watching the kind-hearted family. They overlooked her oddities, and it seemed that they cherished her even more for all she didn't know. Nixi was thankful for the family's embrace and patience. When she would do something foolish, they were quick and gentle in rectifying her actions. The family captivated her so much that she had almost forgotten her dreams.

Nixi had been with the family for roughly a week when Agda woke her.

"I need to go to the market today. Would you like to join us?" Nixi was groggy from the slumber, but Agda's warm smile shook her out of her stupor. She ate some breakfast and got ready for the day. When she was ready, Sophia grabbed her hand and escorted her outside. The town was bright, and the smell of the sea was overwhelming. For a brief moment, she missed the home she knew, but even in this short time, she had experienced so much Nixi didn't know if she would return home if she could. She often wondered if Tiberius' family took her in because he could feel her calling even in silence. If that was the case, she was thankful that he had gotten caught in the crossfire of her voice. Sophia escorted Nixi from vendor to vendor. Pointing out things she liked and sometimes even telling her how an item worked if Sophia found it interesting enough to explain. Agda only went to specific vendors and paid no mind to what Sophia was doing, knowing Nixi was by her side. She was more relaxed since Nixi first arrived, and many people she saw took note.

When the day was approaching evening, the vendors had all but packed up, and they returned home. Tiberius was cooking some fish, and the smell made Nixi salivate. She preferred raw fish, but the family had told her that was unacceptable because it was weird. Not just because of the rawness of the fish but also because of how she ate fish. When eating, she was feral, so the family often asked themselves where such a beautiful and wild girl would come from. Nixi followed Sophia to her area, and Sophia would show her a new treasure with every return. Today it was her favorite pebble of the day. It was smooth and grey, matching the other perfect stones Sophia had found on other outings. When dinner was ready, Tiberius called for the girls to come to the table, so Sophia and Nixi meandered to dinner. When Nixi got past the curtain that separated Sophia's space from the kitchen, she was dumbstruck. At the table stood a fair man whom she immediately recognized as Dorus. Like a shock to her system, Nixi remembered the trials and tribulations she had endured to meet him. How could she have forgotten about him? A lot had happened to Nixi in the past few weeks, and all those cherished memories stepped back into the recesses of her mind. She only had one thought now, and that thought was of Dorus.

She politely sat down across from him, and when he looked at her, she gave a soft smile and nod. She became nervous in her actions, and her face flushed. "This is the girl I told you about. She had been staying with us for a while now. She's been such a blessing to our house. I wanted to introduce you two." Dorus looked at the girl and returned the smile.

"Hello, I am Dorus, and you are?" Sophia cut through the shared glance.

"She likes to be called Nixi.. because she's a pixie!" Tibierius pat Sophia's head laughing. "She can't talk, but I know what she says." Sophia continued pulling back her shoulders, taking a proud stance. She then grabbed some bread and handed it to Nixi. Nixi graciously took the bread and added it to the plate that Agda placed in front of her. Though she tried to avoid it, her eyes drifted to Dorus, and when her eyes met his, she would look down at her plate again. He was more attractive up close than he had been with a sheet of water between the two.

When Dorus saw Nixi, he felt time stand still. When Tiberius told him about a girl they had taken under their wing, he thought the girl would be around Sophia's age, but the girl was a young woman and no longer a child. He knew she was mute when he agreed to meet the guest that had taken the household like a storm in rocky waters. All their time and attention had turned to this woman, and he could finally understand why they had turned their worlds upside down for her. Nixi was striking and pliant. She was youthful but had a way about her that seemed almost wise. Maybe it was just the fact that she couldn't speak. Either way, Dorus was ready to fill the void of her voice with all the words he wished she'd say. Dorus stared at the girl, unafraid of catching her eye. When he succeeded, she would quickly look away, and it ached his heart to not be devoured by her stare. He was aroused in a way he had never known before. He did not want to chase her. Instead, he desired to lay down his life and be devoured by her. There were not enough words in his vocabulary to recite how he wanted to make the girl happy. She was everything he knew he wanted but was only now aware of. The night ended, and Dorus and Tiberius went for their weekly walk.

"How enchanting she is!" He exclaimed when he knew she would not hear him. Tiberius chuckled.

"On that, we can both agree!" Dorus had heard Tiberius talk about the stranger that took up his residence, and it was because of how eager Tiberius and his family were to appease her that he had to meet her. He worried that his friend was being taken advantage of. Now he realized that they had been taking advantage of her. Her mere presence was intoxicating.

"Do you think she would be willing to be courted by me?" He asked Tiberius in earnest.

"I cannot give you promises that are not mine to make. I have no reason to have a dowry about her. You, my friend, are free to ask her if you were to cultivate a wife of her. If she accepts, then I would be happy for you both."

Dorus understood that she had nothing to her name. No title, no riches, and to those that required status above all things would not be taken by such a girl with as many words as she had pocket change. He had thought up until this very night that he would settle for a woman of status that rivaled his own. His childhood upbringing brought Tiberius into his life, and it was only by that single thread that they became lifelong friends. Tiberius knew his friend held a future of that of a king if not for the senate. He knew his friend had a world that he would never understand. Dorus had his choice of women with large dowries and even more extensive opportunities. Many well-to-do fathers had pushed their very attractive, often intolerable well-bred women in his path, and the thought of Dorus settling down with a vagrant tickled Tiberius with a proud spite at those more fortunate than he.

Tiberius was happy with his simple life, but the future that Dorus's family could afford had, on occasion, brought a fit of sad jealousy in him. He thought about Nixi. She would be wise to entertain Dorus as a mate, and once more, he felt the ping of jealousy. This time not due to his friend's fortune but the idea of losing Nixi from his household. She had brought joy to his family and fulfilled a place in their hearts that he could not fully express. The thought of her moving on from him made his heart ache and would possibly break his wife's and, furthermore, Sophia's hearts. They had become as attached to her as Tiberius found himself when his dear friend spoke of luring her away. As a sensible man, Tiberius knew that it would be in her interest to wed a man like Dorus and that the loss that would ripple through the core of his family could not stand in the way of it.

"I can ask her on the matter of courting, but I must warn you, my dear friend, she will always have a place in our household, so she is in no immediate need of a suitor. I will gladly stand in your way at her request." Tiberius jumped in front of his friend, mimicking holding a sword. Dorus laughed.

"We need not shed blood over the matter! There is something about her that even if she declined my offer, I would not feel ashamed for having tried!" Tiberius put his arm around Dorus, and they laughed. As both were elated at the idea of Nixi's future.

The following afternoon Dorus showed up at Tiberius's house with a basket of bread and eggs. He wanted to offer Nixi something as he requested some of her time, and as he had initially decided on flowers, sadly, no bud could translate to the beauty he perceived from her. He thought of the countless men who, in a quest for her affections, had brought her flowers and decided that he needed to do something to separate him from the rest. So he chose bread because he had seen her enjoy bread at their meal. He also bought some eggs to appeal to Sophia's senses. He thought that Sophia and Nixi were practically inseparable, so gaining her goodwill would help his chances. On his way to their house, he saw a wildflower and, as an afterthought, added it to the basket. Just in case, Nixi enjoyed such things. When Dorus knocked on the door, Agda opened the door. Upon seeing Dorus with a gift in hand, she smiled brightly, and it was apparent that she and Tiberius had whiled away the hours talking on the subject. She called out to Nixi, all the while smiling at Dorus.

Sophia first arrived at the door as Nixi slowly followed. When Sophia saw the basket, she exclaimed,

"Is that for us!" She then proceeded to unburden Dorus of the basket.

"It's actually for Nixi!" he called out, but Sophia had disappeared into the house. Dorus sighed at his loss of presentation. Would Nixi even get to see any of the gifts that Dorus had brought? He smiled through his annoyance but forgot about it when Nixi took his hand and bowed to him. An acceptance of the present, he was assured by Agda. Dorus stood tall once more:

"Would you be interested in exploring the town with me?"

Nixi smiled and could feel her cheeks redden. She didn't understand why she was so easy to fluster when he was around, but she was thrilled to be around him. She nodded to the offer of a walk and his time. Dorus held out his hand, and as Nixi moved hers to fall into his, Sophia appeared from the shadows taking Dorus's hand.

"I'm so excited to explore the city with you!" She began to drag him to the road. Nixi smiled vibrantly; if she could, she would have laughed at the moment that escaped her. Dorus saw the smile and laughed on her behalf. Agda looked at Nixi before pushing her out the door.

"You best follow them, or Sophia may steal him from you!" Nixi ran to catch up to the pair.

Dorus showed up every day after to invite Nixi for a walk. Sophia would always insist on joining them. Still, they had moments. Sometimes Dorus would point at something and place his other hand on the small of her back. Each time a wave of thrill would befall her. Other times as they walked, he would get close, and his hand would brush hers. Hungry to touch one another. When Sophia saw this, she would break their contact and have them hold her hands instead. Then they would walk hand in hand, Nixi, Sophia, and Dorus. With Sophia in the middle as much as she was able. Although Nixi was desperate to be in Dorus's arms, she was thankful for the child keeping them at bay. She wanted to know him beyond just the feelings she had carried for him since her first excursion to the town.

Chapter 10: Unraveled

Four months after Nixi left her home for her grand adventure, her sisters became worried. She hadn't given so much as a goodbye note due to the sea witch's instruction. Each of her sisters traveled to where she might have been, but there was no trace of her. Two months after the young mermaid's disappearance, Despoine asked Triton to see if he could find her. He, after all, was the most capable among them, having a mirror image of his father's powers. Triton called on several whales to comb the sea for his beloved sister. After a month, all of the whales had returned empty-handed.

The sisters were beside themselves because being unable to find Nixi likely meant that she was captured by the realm of man. If that was the case, she would surely be dead, as it was rumored that consuming a mermaid's tail was an aphrodisiac, and consuming its heart granted you one wish with no limits on what could be asked. A mountain of gold? Easy. A dead one brought back to life? Not unheard of. A wish for more wishes? Quite possibly. They all took turns going to the harbor that she would frequent, and when they saw the man in which she pined, he was bright, cheery, and acting like he had no care in the world. They had decided that with that much joy, it could only be brought on by consuming Nixi's heart. So the sisters took it upon themselves to send crabs to claw at him and urged birds to bring chaos to his life. They saw him often walking with a girl who seemed able to deflect all attacks on the man. Through the shimmering waters, none of her sisters recognized her as the sister for which they searched.

It was eight months after Nixi's disappearance, Kymopoleia entered Amphitrites' part of the castle. It was well known that Amphitrite did not care for the children who were not sprung from her womb, but Kymopoleia was desperate for revenge. As soon as she entered the room, she could practically choke on Amphitrite's irritation at her presence.

"I'm sorry, grandmother, but I kindly ask for a word with you?" Her voice shook with fear as she approached the woman that carried so much disdain for her. If Kymopoleia could have let it go, she would have, but she could not.

"I'm sure you are aware that Nixi has gone missing. I fear she is dead. Eaten by a human man. I humbly ask for your help seeking revenge for my departed sister?" She posed every request to Amphitrite as a question to gain favor from the goddess.

Amphitrite unfurled herself. One octopus tentacle lifted from another until they released her, and she changed into a humanoid form. She often took a human shape in the castle to show her superiority. She could walk with the humans just as well as the creatures of the sea and was known as the only one other than Poseidon able to take whatever form she pleased without hesitation. She took that of a beautiful long-legged woman. Causing jealousy in all the creatures of the sea who often desperately wished for the same skill to get out of trouble if caught in a net. Kymopoleia was awestruck at the sight of the woman she called grandmother. She quickly bent her body in a deep bow as her jaw dropped. So deep that she would have toppled over had it not been for a stroke of luck.

"Where is this man you claim to have taken your sister?" Amphitrite's voice was deep and as enchanting as her visage.

"She had gotten a crush on a human in the Isle of Rhodes. She had seen him when Rhodos introduced her to the island that sprung from her and Helios's love. I fear in her obsession; she was caught. The man seems to have gotten a bout of luck since she had disappeared. We've sent crabs and birds to attack him, but none seem to get to him. I implore you to seek vengeance where I am unable." Amphitrite waved her hands at the now-crying Kymopoleia; it was clear it was time for her to exit.

"Please, grandmother," she choked out before making a hasty exit.

Amphitrite rubbed her temples. She had known of Nixi's disappearance and could not express how much she didn't care about the subject but knew if the likes of Kymopoleia had entered her chamber that all of the children were likely to follow. It was clear from the day she claimed each child that she held no care for them. If they were not her own, they were hoi polloi and did not deserve the audience with herself. Yet here was one begging for revenge for another. She could feel her peace coming to a halt if she didn't nip this Nixi situation in the bud. She crossed the room to approach a black mirror. Much like the pools of Hades, this mirror could show her whatever she wished. She had it made when she decided to never return to Atargatis with the child. She wanted to watch the woman suffer as she did every other person that suffered the same childless fate that Atargatis had. It had been years since she noticed the child she called Nixi. She thought about how delicious it would be to shove her death in Atartgatis's face where she could revel in her misery once more. Amphitrite dreamt about recounting to Atargatis the tale of Nixi dying at the hands of man. The thought alone rushed a vindictive smile to her face.

Amphitrite touched the black pool, thinking of Nixi, and her bright face immediately appeared. Her smile turned downward at the reflection. Nixi was alive and seemed quite well.

"How disappointing." She said to herself. As Amphtrite watched the girl, a child entered the frame, holding her face close to Nixi. It seemed that Nixi was not only alive, but she was thriving.

"I'll have to put a stop to that!" She huffed. The image of Nixi and the child panned out, and she could see Nixi surrounded with adoration. The adoration of.. Humans? She looked at Nixi again, and there she saw it. Nixi was no longer a creature of the sea but had sprouted legs from her caudal fin.

Amphitrite's eyes narrowed.

"Atargatis," she growled. It had to be her doing. She slinked into a lavish chair and watched the story of Nixi unfold. She had been taken in by a human family that seemed to love and care for the child. She saw Nixi go on walks with a good-looking young man with an air of royalty. This must have been the man that Kymopoleia had mentioned. He looked as enamored as Nixi obviously was. Amphitrite's hands balled up in fists as rage began to seep into her every crevice. She had not taken Nixi so that she may have a good and prosperous life. Nixi needed to suffer for Atargatis' sake. She had the mirror follow the man that Nixi admired.

As Nixi, Sophia, and Dorus returned to the house that Nixi was inhabiting, he bowed deeply to Nixi,

"May I see you again tomorrow?" Nixi smiled enthusiastically. Sophia stepped between the two and waved her hand at Dorus.

"I am busy in the morning. Mom and I will go to the market, and Nixi will join us." She turned to stare daggers at Nixi. She bowed her head and smiled softly as if to say okay. Dorus looked at Nixi, his eyes begging her to ditch the market so they might spend some time alone. Nixi looked at him and shrugged before turning to Sophia and taking her hand. Obviously, choosing the child over him. His shoulders sunk in defeat, and he smiled, addressing Sophia.

"Would you like to join me for dinner then?" Sophia triumphantly nodded in agreement and pulled Nixi into the house with her. Nixi looked over her shoulder as she turned her back to Dorus and smiled. She was at the mercy of young Sophia.

Upon the two girls' entrance, Tiberius came out of the house and greeted Dorus.

"Dorus! My friend! I see you've been out with the girls again. Do you have time to walk with your old friend? Or have the girls worn you out?" he chuckled, tapping Sophia's head as she passed him. She was quick to rebuke the tap and hurried the both of them in.

"I would love to catch up with you." Dorus embraced his friend, and they walked to the bridge.

"It looks like you have your choice of the ladies in the house of Tiberius. I can't tell if Sophia is trying to keep an eye on you for Nixi's benefit or her own."

The two men chuckled. "Sophia will resent me when I ask Nixi to be my bride." Tiberius raised an eyebrow.

"It's that time already?" Dorus nodded.

"Yes, I know it may not be so long since we first met, but it has been too long for me. Every moment without her by my side seems like an eternity I can no longer bear."

"Excellent!" Tiberius rejoiced. "When will you make the proposal?"

"The end of the week if I can get a moment alone with her." They both laughed. It was, after all, a more manageable task said than done.

Amphitrite joined them in their laughter as she looked at the pool that showed the exchange.

"What luck!" it was as if the universe was conspiring to her will. She knew that there was a way to impede their nuptials. She just needed to move fast. She packed up some things and went to the town where Dorus lived. It had been a while since she had felt a need to enchant, but it was like riding a horse, and she was confident of her success.

The next day Dorus returned to his home after another elated walk with Nixi and Sophia. His heart pounded hard and fast at the idea of being wed to Nixi. He felt like he could sing all about it, but he was not a man of song. His mother, Hellen, was quick to greet him.

"Dorus! Finally, you're here!" She quickly hugged the young man kissing him on the cheek.

"What has got you all riled up?" He smiled. He loved when his mother fawned over him, but she never did it unless she wanted something once he reached adulthood. His mother squealed.

"I don't know if you remember my childhood friend Vasaliki?" Dorus nodded yes, but he could not recall ever hearing about a woman of that name. "Well, she and her daughter, Jumana, have just arrived for a visit. Jumana," His mother contently sighed, "What a good omen!"

The name meant pearl and was the business where his family had found much wealth. He had spent his formative years in the East learning how to cultivate the precious pebbles before returning home to expand on his parents' wealth. Dorus rolled his eyes at the idea of a name being a good omen, but he was always willing to humor his mother in her lavish superstitions. She corralled Dorus into the courtyard. There an older woman sat fanning herself, and a woman about his age quietly stood. When the young woman looked up, Dorus was taken aback. He had never seen such beauty and was instantly entranced by the Arabic woman. He now understood that his mother had been friends with the woman by business alone. They had probably known each other through trade circles in his father's business.

"Isn't she beautiful!" Hellen fawned. "She's looking for a husband. Just imagine how fortuitous it would be if you secured our standing with that family." Dorus looked at his mother. She had known of his affection for Nixi and his intentions, but obviously, his mother had other plans.

"What are you trying to do, mother?" He said cautiously.

"You are ready to marry, so I have made this favorable match. Our merger with this family would ensure happiness throughout your family's line. She is significantly fairer than your current infatuation." The last word she said flatly to show her distaste for his union to Nixi. "Just give her a week and see if your favor can be reconsidered. One week, no visits to see that girl, and if you look twice and are set in your notion, then who am I to stand in your way" I'm just a mother who wants her son to be happy, but love can be fleeting, and when it does, don't you want something to fall back on?" She caressed Dorus's face and then smacked it twice.

"You can give your poor tired mother one week, can't you? Surely there is no need to hop on the first opportunity you see? Pretty faces are often cheap. On the other hand, Jumana has everything a man like you should ever want!" Dorus sighed in defeat.

One week to entertain this woman so his mother would be appeased didn't seem unreasonable. He approached Jumana and bowed at her.

"Welcome to the Isle of Rhodes. We look forward to showing you the highlights of our beloved isle." Jumana smiled at him,

'What a captivating woman,' he thought.

When he had submitted to entertaining for the week, Hellen and Vasaliki headed indoors, chatting with one another, leaving Dorus and Jumana alone.

"It is good to meet you," she said. Her voice was smooth and rich. She really was a beauty. He bowed to her and said,

"In the morning, we will take out a chariot, and I can show you around." Jumana smiled brightly at the young man. He excused himself for the evening. For a second, he worried that being in Jumana's presence might change his perspective, and that scared him more than anything ever had. Could he love two women? What a mess he had found himself in.

When his mother and Vasaliki found themselves alone, Hellen threw herself to the ground before Vasaliki.

"Thank you, Amphitrite, for giving my son this opportunity! I am sure he will make the right decision for us both." Amphitrite helped the woman off the floor.

"The pleasure is mine. You have been devout to the gods, and we have heard your pleas. When the consummation with Jumana is completed, Aphrodite will bless you with tears of happiness and ensure your future is filled with wealth and endless joy." Hellen cried out with enthusiasm. Her son had caught the eye of the gods and blessed their house. She was elated and ready to do anything to solidify their future.

"I will return for the wedding between young Jumana and Dorus in a week. Ensure the other woman who has caught his eye is prevented from swaying your son on the topic of this merger." Hellen nodded.

"I assure you I will." With that vow, Amphitrite took leave of Hellen and returned to the sea. She had a sea witch to deal with.

Chapter 11: Reunited

As Amphitrite descended into the depths of the sea, she noted how much darker the realm seemed than her memory recalled. It had been one hundred eighty years since her last dive into the area and one hundred years since she bothered to look in on Atargatis via her black pool. She had grown bored of watching Atargatis suffer but had always taken solace in knowing about her cruel fate. There had been moments that Amphitrite had thought about looking in on her, but often something else would pull her thoughts from Atargatis, and she would divert her attention, having come up with a more entertaining subject to watch. Amphitrite wondered if the land had always been so dark or had the darkness expanded with time. She had even seen a few new species of sea creatures that she had not been previously aware of. 'Time changes all.' she thought bitterly. Somehow, she had seen the world change, but it never crossed her mind that this place might also alter itself from the desolate land that once was.

She had worried that with all the years that had slipped by, she might be unable to find the cave where she was once imprisoned. When she saw a grotto, she looked into them to verify they were not the place she was looking for. For a moment, she wondered if Atargatis had even stayed in the cave after eighty years. She had been the prisoner to no one save herself, so she had no reason to stay in one location. Amphitrite told herself that if Atargatis had moved on, she would track her down and restore her suffering. She didn't feel the need to maintain Atargatis' suffering anymore, but it was the principle. If she let her meddle with her child's affairs, she might find the fortitude to seek revenge, and that was something that Amphitrite could not stand for. The more she swam, the more her passion for Atartgatis' struggles renewed her interest. Once more, she was devoured by the idea of making her enemy suffer.

Amphitrite felt accomplished when she came upon a familiar cavern opening. She knew at once that she was where she had desired to be. Entering the cave, Amphitrite transformed into an octopus-inspired body. As of late, it had been her favorite shape to be because she could multitask without much thought. The tentacles also took up a lot of space, making her presence overwhelmingly foreboding. Her tentacles wrapped up the cave walls as she propelled herself slowly forward. Every pebble and crevice in the room was thoroughly explored as she progressed deeper into the location where Atargatis and Amphitrite's fates had first crossed. Amphitrite noted the cavern had become more chasmic as time had lapsed. Had Amphitrite expanded the area with her settling in?

One of Amphitrite's tentacles had found something. It explored the object, and once it was confirmed as a movable, she pulled it from the ground and placed it into the hands that still remained on her body. It was a little glass bottle. Empty and without a top. Evidence that Atargatis had nested and made the hole in the wall home. Her hand wrapped around the bottle, and she squeezed until the bottle crumbled into shards and dispersed back onto the floor in pieces. As she passed over them, she had begun filling her heart with angry spite. How dare Atargatis find a beacon of light in the darkness.

Amphitrite progressed further down the gallery finding more discarded trinkets cluttering the path. She made a point to destroy each object she happened upon, leaving a sharp, dangerous trail in Amphitrite's wake.

She noted the dimly lit room as the gallery opened to an underground chamber. There were all kinds of bottles and sordid items carefully placed in the recesses of the chamber. Making shelves to hold the bits of debris in a way that likely had an order, Amphitrite was sure she could figure out if she spent the time on it. In one area, there was a black pool that was much like her own. It was an item made solely for the trinity gods, Poseidon, Hades, and Zeus. How could Atargatis have access to one? Had Poseidon returned to the arms of Atargatis and bestowed gifts to her? The thought fed her disgust, she knew that Atargatis had been playing her with tales of woe when she spoke of her husband, finally, she had proof and she slid back into her long-dormant hatred for Atargatis.

Atargatis was having a fairly uneventful day. Her only objective of the day was to help a phoeocna sinus couple get pregnant and check in on Nixi. The couple had been pleading their case to Atargatis. They had not yet conceived any children despite regular attempts. Overcome with an exacerbation of their failure. In tears, they had found Atargatis. A creature in the darkest depths of the sea known to facilitate any creature's fertility to their favor. It brought Atargatis joy to facilitate the accomplishment of the dreams of others. Often her only charge had been ingredients that she may need to make a potion for the couple to partake. Occasionally, she asked for something a bit more obscure, but she wanted to help others. Today was no different. After she heard the couple's pleas, she went to her shelves, pulling one item after the next as the couple laid some horse hairs on the table in the middle of the room that Atargatis had requested. It was not the easiest thing to come across. Upon a visit to Poseidon's principal dwelling, they cultivated the item from the gods' stables and returned to Atargatis with a renewed hope brimming from their hearts.

As Atargatis finished the fabrication of the fertility potion, she turned around to face the hopeful couple but was immediately distracted by a prominent ominous figure in the chamber's doorway. Immediately everything about Atargatis' nature changed. Her warm smile fell flat, and her head bowed in disappointment. She was quick to excuse the couple from her domicile. The two phoeocna sinuses, brimming with hope, made their way to the exit. They were surprised when they turned around to exit to see a member of royalty, known as a goddess of the sea, filling up the space of the doorway. Amphitrite's face was stoic, and she paid no attention to the couple as they passed. Her eyes fixated on Atargatis. The couple quickly swam from the cage, and as they exited, they were filled with renewed excitement. A goddess was a client of Atargatis. If that was the case, then they were sure that the potency of the potion they were advised to take would yield great results.

Atargatis produced two drinks and placed them at the table before sitting in front of one while pushing the other toward Amphitrite. A gesture that was an invitation for Amphitrite to join her for a cup of whatever murky fluid Atargatis had provided and a seat.

"It's been a while," Atargatis said with a somber tone that didn't seem to be directed at anyone. Amphitrite approached the table but did not sit down. She wanted to loom over Atargatis so that she would recognize that Atargatis would always be below her.

"It's come to my attention that you've been meddling in human affairs." Her tentacles still searched the room as she loomed over the calm Atargatis.

"Maybe a tad." her voice was quiet, but Amphitrite swore there was a hint of defiance in it with a subtle teasing nature. Hearing that defiance ignited Amphitrite's anger.

Who did she think she was treating her that way? Her eyes meandered to the black pool.

"You need to call Nixi back to the sea and reverse the trouble you've caused." Atargatis broke through the dense atmosphere with an unbridled laugh, further inciting Amphitrite's anger.

"It's been one hundred eighty years since you TOOK my child." She had a heavy emphasis on the theft of her child.

"Oh, give me a break," Amphitrite growled. "You gave me that child. Just because you lived to regret it doesn't make me a thief. I cared for her, raised her in comfort, and gave her a life outside the squalor you would have provided. You should grovel and thank me for all I did for that blemish of the sea." Upon receipt of the perspective, Atargatis became inflamed and pulled herself away from the table with a loud smack as her hand hit it.

"You took away all I have. Why? I thought we were friends. Then for no apparent reason, you destroyed what little I had. Why? Why? It's my most dwelt-upon thought, and I still don't understand why."

"Look at you. Born to play the victim," Amphitrite retorted. "You like to play innocent, but you are not. You lapped up my husband's affections and expected me to sit idly by. My husband may not be a great man, but he is far better than to deserve the likes of you."

Atargatis' mouth dropped. 'Lapped up his affections?' She never had a desire for Poseidon in any period of her timeline. How delusional was this woman before her who she repeatedly told tales of the pain, hardships, and rapes that Posiedon indulged himself with at her expense? How could Amphitrite endorse her trauma when Atargatis only dreamt of escape. Amphitrite, at any point, could have released her from the prison Poseidon had put her in but actively made excuses for her departure. All she had wanted was to return to her beaches and mourn the loss of her love. She had endured everything else because she had thought she deserved it after Adad's passing. Atargatis ached with every fiber of her being. Although back then, a part of her felt she deserved to be punished for the death of her one and only love, she had paid her penance for Adad's tragedy.

Atargatis filled with rage. A rage she had been stifling since she entered these hostile waters.

"It's fine. I've already started to clean up your mess." Amphitrite said coolly, brushing a strand of hair from her face. "Nixi will be back where she belongs shortly, I am sure."

"What have you done?" Atargatis said as her hand became a fist. Amphitrite moved over to the black pool, sticking her finger in it. From the ripples, Dorus' face appeared.

"Me?" Amphitrite said innocently, but Atargatis could feel the taunting subtext making her rage grow.

"I merely gave him another choice of wife. A woman more suited to him and his family's agenda. Gods are known for giving humans favorable lives when well deserved. I am helping some generous humans with a bit of benevolence and a dash of incentive." Amphitrite tried to keep a placid face but a wicked smile emerged from the corner of her mouth.

"I wouldn't be surprised if the courting had already turned into a proposal for my smart match." Several of Amphitrites' tentacles had wrapped themselves around the table at which Atargatis had been sitting. She removed her finger from the black pool, and the image of Dorus disappeared.

"I guess I should return home. I'm expecting a severely distraught Nixi to return to my doorstep, and I will have an opportunity to console her, or maybe.." Amphitrite paused, "Maybe I'll have to exile her for meddling with humans. I haven't decided."

Amphitrite turned to face the exit. As she did, her tentacles that had been exploring the table lifted it and flung it into the black pool, destroying Atargatis' window to any world than the darkness she had been sequestered to. The table did not stop at the pool as Amphitrite flung the table at the shelves next. Leaving nothing but destruction in her wake.

Atargatis fell into the pool. She had never felt so angry and, yet, so helpless. Her window to her daughter was no more, and the aftermath of her home echoed a similar future for her beloved daughter. She gathered anything she could salvage from the wreckage of her home and made her way to the harbor she had seen so many times in her reflection pool. Atargatis emerged from her destruction with a new conviction. She would have to return to the land of humans and save her child from a fate that would break her. She could not let her child pay for the sins of the mother. She would not only have to embrace the person she once was but would also have to expose herself by shedding the person she had tried to become. Atargatis would do this by manifesting all her anger and becoming the person that Amphitrite had feared all along. It was, after all, the least she could do for her beloved daughter.

Chapter 12: The Meeting

Nixi hung her feet off the dock that, not so long ago, she had watched Dorus sit upon. Her legs did not reach the water, so her toes hovered a few inches above the water. Only a few inches separated her from a world she had abandoned. A world she wished with all her being she could return to. She watched boats pass by, thinking of the choices she had made. How could she be so foolish and naive? She thought she was an adult and didn't want to be told that she was making decisions for the young. She had given up everything, and now she sat alone the night before the love of her life was to wed. She thought about the tales her sisters had told her about humans and mermaids not mixing. She was confident that she would be the exception. Now she was going to have to accept that she wasn't.

The thoughts turned over in her mind and became ravaged in despair. It all happened so fast. One day, she awoke with foolish dreams, and Dorus had been waiting for her. He had sat her down and told her he had planned to wed another. Devastated silence swept over her. She had wanted nothing more than Dorus to be happy. She had, however, always assumed that she would be the one to stand by him for his happily ever after. She wasn't the one for him. The thoughts felt bitter in her gut. Maybe her loss of love was a hard lesson learned. There could be other men on land and perhaps even the sea if she could figure out how to return to the waters she called home. She had options; she just had no desire to accept them. She wanted the love of Dorus and no other. She would have to spend the rest of eternity wishing she hadn't lost him.

Tears sprung from her eyes like a geyser. Her hands cupped her face, and she momentarily pulled away to see her palms soaked in tears. 'Human tears.' she thought. She had heard about it but never experienced it. She only knew Kymopoleia to cry, but each tear she shed turned into a sand dollar, a curse upon her. She wondered if all sea creatures could cry wet tears and didn't know about it. In the story of Oceanus, as he fell to pieces, his tears filled each body of water. Did he cry these waters? Were mermaids supposed to drown in the sorrow but learned to adapt? Or were these tears a mark of the sacrifice she had made? The pain renewed as she thought about everything she had given up. Her family, culture, and life only to embrace something as pointless as unrequited love.

Nixi watched the tears trickle through her fingertips and fall into the same ocean she once called home. She fantasized about turning back the hands of time. If she could, she would have never explored the surface waters. She would have never loved and would be living a carefree ignorant life she was once privy. She would have never traded her life for these silly legs if only she could turn back time. She looked at them in disgust. She could not return to her oceanic bedroom and dream of her life unknown. She would not be wallowing in the pain and heartache she found herself in.

She then thought of a solution. What if she just jumped and let the water take her? She knew she wouldn't be able to return home as a mermaid. She also knew that despite watching humans swim, she had yet to be successful in the endeavor. People always looked like they were flailing about and somehow magically stayed afloat. She just found herself sinking no matter how hard she tried to mimic the humans in the water. She knew swimming was a beacon of life, and sinking meant humans would drown and descend to the bottom, where life was stripped from their bodies. She had feared that same fate. So she remained in shallow waters since becoming one of them.

The wood beneath her was cool and damp. She could feel bits of the wood fray, and a splinter threatened her with a new discomfort. She then took a big breath in, slightly choking on tears that had yet to make their debut. Inhaling to the maximum capacity of her lungs, she could taste the air. She noted the flavorful scents of wet oak, sweat, alcohol, salt, and fish. She made sure to appreciate the smell that had engaged other senses. She closed her eyes and let the sound of water lapping banks fill her with peace. This moment of breathing air would exhilarate her sisters. None of them were able to relish this moment because they could not survive above the surface. She could imagine them bright-eyed, gathered around her, waiting with bated breath to hear the tale of humanity. She loved all the experiences she had had in this human body. It was new, refreshing, and exhilarating. Now she had the rest of her life to experience it all.

She slid off the dock into the water. Holding onto the pier to keep her from sinking too deep into the water. She wanted to be in the water because she felt the comfort of her home there. When she let go, she began to sink, and against her wish to do so, she flailed around, searching for the dock's easement once more. Water flooded her mouth as she tried to get air into her lungs. She grabbed the port again and, pulling herself as high as possible, inched toward the banks. The ocean was an enemy. She didn't belong to the land, nor was she welcomed in the sea any longer. Without her love and family, she was just a composition of poor decisions. It was too late to change her mind. She was losing her will to fight. She was ready to end it all but did not want to go out in fear. She thought about her family, friends, and, most importantly, Dorus. She closed her eyes and found calm. Her arms relaxed, and she once more began to sink into the water's warm embrace.

She gasped for another breath but found herself inhaling the water and began to slip away, finally living up to her destiny. She was hardly conscious when she felt something take her, pushing her to shore before passing out. When Nixi's eyes opened, she saw stars and clouds above her. As her senses became more explicit, she became aware of the water still filling her mouth and began to choke on it, trying to regurgitate the salty water. She bolted into an upright position and went to cover her mouth. Instead of her hand cupping her mouth, she had briskly thrown sand into it, giving her even more opportunity to choke. She spat out the grainy sludge that had replaced the excess water in her mouth. She noticed a figure to her left and slowly turned toward it. There sat a woman who was gazing out to the sea. Though she was clear of scales and other ocean-bound features, Nixi recognized her as the sea witch. She, however, no longer had a hag-like appearance but was captivating with long, flowing black hair, but there was something oddly familiar about her that Nixi could not place like the remnants of a good dream. Nixi wondered, with a human visage like hers, why she had resigned herself to the sea where she spent her time homely and alone.

"You know, I was once in love." The witch said aloud, not to Nixi specifically, a confession to the universe. Nixi was silent. "I was a maiden, maybe even a goddess, but one day, my lover was gone. There was no rhyme or reason, but I was wildly in love, and then there was nothing but a gaping hole in my chest where my heart used to be. When he passed, I was decidedly going to follow. My life without him was vacant and empty, and I thought if I could escape into death, maybe one day I could be reunited with him. So I resolved to drown myself. The gods had other plans. One of them desired me and wanted me as his concubine. I had no interest, but none can deny the whims of the gods, so I had no choice but to submit."

"It soon came to light that I was with child. I thought with the entirety of my being that the child belonged to my deceased lover. Sadly, I could not prove it to be so. When the beautiful child was purged from my body, the god's wife took her from me. A punishment for gaining a god's favor. Losing my lover was hard, but it paled compared to losing my child. I found myself in uncharted waters and made it my home. Hoping that if I stay someday, my child might discover me. "

'Did they return?' Nixi questioned by making movements of her hands, enthralled with the story. Atargatis smiled.

"She did. It was the happiest day of my life. She didn't recognize me. Maybe she never knew her mother to be anyone other than the one who raised her. She had found her way because she needed to find a way to make the impossible possible. I could not say no. I had waited so long to be able to be there for my darling daughter. It would cost me everything. If I took on the impossible task and succeeded, I would never see her again, but I knew I brought her happiness. If I failed, I would never see her again, and she would associate me with disappointment. Which for me was a more dismal fate. So I disarmed her." Nixi had a questioning look on her face. Atargatis nodded. "She had a curse that her voice would bring madness to the land of man. Her voice was an addiction, and humans were designed to follow her to their death if life was kind to them and to madness if they were to suffer. So I took her voice so she wouldn't condemn her lover to death."

Nixi's eyes grew wide as she pieced together this woman's story with a tale that Triton used to tell. Nixi knew that she was not the daughter of Amphitrite, but it was an unspoken fact that she rarely ever gave a thought to. Every once in a while, when Triton and Nixi were alone, he would tell her the tale of a woman who had given birth to her, but he had stories for all his sisters. She was willing to die for love, but Poseidon would not let that happen. The woman must have been something special to have a god intervene in her life. Although he knew that the woman would never truly love him like she had loved the man she was set to follow, he took her in and cared for her, despite it. The story ended with Poseidon's heartbreak. The woman he had tried to save did not love him as she had before and left without a trace leaving her daughter discarded until Poseidon and Amphitrite took her in as one of their own. Nixi had never felt like one of theirs. She and several sisters would often be cast aside in light of one of the children they favored, a silent claim to be theirs.

Nixi sat slack-jawed as she recalled her history and merged it with this new information. Was this woman who sat beside her the same mother who had abandoned her so long ago? Discarded and unwanted. Now she is talking about staying in the cavern that was her home waiting for her? She was flooded with a myriad of emotions, but confusion was the most prominent of the lot. Nixi had so much to say to this woman. Inundated with so many whys. She opened her mouth, but once more, there was only silence.

"You still can't talk. I didn't want you to destroy your love and everyone in the city. Even the lightest whisper can turn a human into a creature of obsession. The madness will grow and eventually result in death."

Atargatis abruptly turned her whole body to Nixi, making eye contact.

"I needed you to know your history so that you could forgive me for all that I have done and all that I have failed. I have a history with Amphitrite. It is a long story that not even I fully understand. It is why you can not speak to humans without them paying with their life. It was ensured that you will always be tied to the sea, but the sea is not where you belong. It is just where you ended up. She may love you," Atargatis fibbed, trying to save Nixi's feelings, "but she wants me to suffer, and I fear it is because of this that you are in the position where you find yourself." She took Nixi's hands in hers and looked into Nixi's eyes. Nixi noted how mournful and tired Atargatis's eyes were. They were almost entirely black. Maybe because she lived in such darkness, she had not been accustomed to the light. She wondered if the moon shining down on them was overbearing to the woman who sat before her.

"Amphitrite knows you are here. She has enchanted the man you love. His love for this other lady is a farce to make you return home. I don't know how to save you from Amphitrite's wrath. Please, if you should do one thing that I ask. I beg of you to not follow in my footsteps." She gestured to the dock that held the waters Nixi had previously tried to drown herself in.

Atargatis stood up as shaky as Nixi had been when she first adjusted to her legs.

"I'm sure you want to get back to your love." Atargatis put out her hand to Nixi in an offer to help her up, and Nixi was happy to accept it. "Your options are limited. You must break the enchantment that Dorus is under. The easiest way is to decapitate his bride. With her dead, the spell is no more. There is a token that also connects them, and destroying that would sever their ties, but that is hard to find as it could be anything and likely requires time that you do not have." Atargatis pulled a button from thin air and placed it in Nixi's hand.

"Or you can swallow this button, and it will turn you into what you really are, and his enchantment will be over. You can then call him to your side, resulting in his death, or you can swim away. He will live to old age, and you will likely never see him again." urgency was in Atargatis' demeanor, and Nixi thought about how she would never be able to decapitate anyone.

"You must be aware of your surroundings if you choose this path, as you will no longer be able to breathe out of the water. I know this is not the ending you thought it would be, but I am behind you no matter the choice you make."

The sun was about to break the horizon's surface, and Atargatis squinted in the light.

"Time for me to go," she smiled. Atargatis returned to the water, changing shape to the haggard sea witch she had first met. The crone turned back to Nixi.

"I'm sorry I never got the chance to watch you grow up, but there was not, and will never ever be a day that I don't think about you. I've only ever wanted all of your dreams to come true. I am sorry I didn't fight hard enough to keep you in my arms." As Atargatis returned to the ocean, she thought about how in this last moment with her daughter, she was still keeping secrets and withholding information from Nixi. The fact was that Nixi's death would also end any enchantments to her, but Atargatis could not risk losing Nixi again. Her head then submerged in the waters, leaving no trace that she had even been there. Nixi would have thought it was all a dream if she hadn't held this round wooden button in her palm.

Nixi sat on the beach for the next half hour, shivering from the cold of her wet clothes that clung desperately to her skin, staring at the button and thinking of her future. She could swallow it now and slip into the sea. No one would know. She would be a memory, and Dorus would continue with his life. Would he even miss her? She hoped that he would. She thought about killing the new bride of Dorus and them being together, but just thinking about it gave her a sick feeling of guilt. Could she live in that guilt forever? Would that moment haunt her, consuming her so that she could spend time with a man she barely knew? She shuttered at the thought.

She could swallow the button in front of Dorus. Transforming into the creature she was. Saving him from a marriage of convenience so that he could love again. Maybe she would do it at their wedding, being far enough away from the waters that had held her lifeline. A sacrifice wedged into Dorus's mind. Would he cry over her dead body, consumed in the loss of his one true love that she was? What if he didn't return her love and she was mistaken? Her last vision of him was in disgust that he had ever shared the air with such a creature knowing all of her choices led to doom. She got up and went to Tiberius' house, tip-toeing to the space she had been calling home.

Tiberius rustled as he made his way into the kitchen. He looked at Nixi and looked at the door. An invitation to spend time with her host, a man learning to live with the madness she had carelessly placed upon him. A pang of guilt struck her heart. Would he try to follow her into the sea if she returned to her ordinary life? She followed him outside as soon as she had put on some dry clothes. When he saw her pass the threshold, he began to walk down the street. Nixi was quick to keep up.

"Long night?" Nixi nodded, but her head sank lower with each bob of her head. "Is this about Dorus?" He gave her a teasing smile, and she nodded, a tiny smile crossing her face as his name was spoken. She blushed lightly.

"You fancied him then?" Nixi made no response.

"Well, I've got to say, I don't like that woman, Jumana, at all! I never thought Dorus would be the type to marry for business. I guess we are all full of surprises." Nixi sighed. Tiberius continued on his one-sided conversation. He wanted to console her but didn't know how. When Dorus had told Tiberius about the union, he seemed different. He spoke with enthusiasm uncharacteristic of his nature. He was sure that Dorus had planned to ask Nixi for her hand. They had discussed the night before, and then the next day, Dorus came to him, telling Tiberius of a woman he loved above all others. In Tiberius' opinion, Jumana didn't have the spark that Dorus had with Nixi. Instead, he pranced around Jumana like a dog lapping for some treats. He then realized that as much as he wanted to comfort Nixi, he didn't know what to say. So he dropped the subject and began to talk about fishing nets. A fascination he often spoke to Nixi about because she had a piece of a net she seemed to cherish. So Tiberius assumed she was partial to them. The morning had become late when Tiberius stopped in his tracks.

"I guess I need to go get ready for the wedding." Just admitting that he was going felt like a betrayal to Nixi. He didn't know why, but he was invested in her affection for Dorus. He needed to see Nixi at her happiest.

"Are you going?" Nixi nodded. "I guess we should both get ready. It's going to be a long day."

Nixi was lost in her thoughts as she walked with Tiberus. She was thinking about family. This man had welcomed her into his family, and she had cherished every minute. She knew a sliver of this acceptance had come about because of a curse. Was their family's kindness only because of an enchantment? She didn't feel like that was the case, but she knew little about humans. She also missed her family. She thought about all of her sisters and the adventures they had had. She thought about her stoic brother Triton who would occasionally tell her stories that would always be outside her own experience. She thought about Poseidon, a god that she got to call father. She thought about her mother, whom she never knew but wanted to. Then she thought of Amphitrite. Was Atargatis being truthful? Had the woman who had raised her been the reason she was not the one to marry her beloved Dorus.

Chapter 13: The Tale Ends

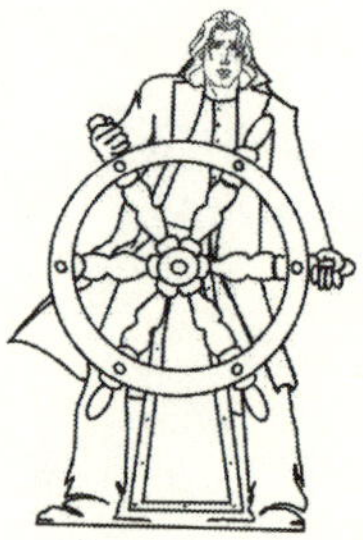

The Tiberius household ascended the ramp to the ship on which the wedding would occur. Nixi was close behind. It was a busy day as most of the town was boarding, so they could see the event of Dorus getting married. There were murmurs about the girl. She came from a wealthy family, and their merger would lead to more prosperity in the village. How could Nixi compete with that? All she had to offer was love. A love that was not returned.

Several townspeople talked about a potential scandal as the wedding was assembled in a hurry, and they were having a wedding in autumn, not the customary winter months. Why were they so desperate to marry now? Nixi felt pity for Jumana. Her new home was not welcoming her with open arms as she had thought they had been for her. She wanted to hate Jumana. After all, she likely didn't love Dorus. They hadn't enough time to explore their feelings. Their parents arranged the union, and the bride and groom were pawns in a game their parents played.

As they entered the ship, Dorus welcomed everyone who had chosen to see the lovely merger. When it was Nixi's turn for his bow, he hesitated.

"I did not expect to see you here." Nixi gave a slight bow to hide her shrug. She didn't know why she was there either. Maybe she needed to see her future with Dorus end. Dorus grabbed Tiberius and pulled him into a hug.

"If she makes a scene, I will hold you accountable," Dorus whispered. Upon hearing the words, Tiberius' face dropped. The thought hadn't even crossed his considerations. Now he was on edge, keeping a careful eye on Nixi. What could he do if she made a scene? He said a little prayer that he would not have to find out. Then they took their seats.

As the ship departed on its journey to the middle of the ocean, the towns folk admired the vast emptiness of the ocean waters, many having never been on a ship before. When Nixi looked out at the horizon, she saw life. She was lost in it as people meandered to the other side of the vessel. There was a commotion, and it attracted all the townsfolk with a murmured excitement.

Someone yelled that the procession was ready, and the people went to their spots to see the event of the year.

The couple stood at the bow, hand in hand, as another man began speaking about the wonders of marriage. When he finished, the couple were presented with a cup to drink from. A sign of their unity, someone in the crowd spoke out before Jumana could raise the cup to her mouth.

"Stop!" The whole ship fell silent as they turned to the woman that had spoken out. The woman stood and began gracefully climbing the stairs to stand with the couple. Nixi's jaw dropped as she recognized the woman as Amphitrite. The commotion that had happened earlier was her arrival, she realized, because she knew she had not arrived before departure. Amphitrite did not like humans and kept her interactions with them as quick as possible. What was she doing here, at this wedding?

Amphitrite gazed out into the crowd looking for something, before raising her hands over her head.

"I have hand-picked the union between these two. With their union, the wealth of both families will increase, and all its townspeople will have my favor because of this merger" There were hushed voices from the people in the hull of the ship.

"No wonder they were so quick to marry."

"We all get to benefit, and Dorus being the honorable man he is, must have expedited the union."

"Thank the gods."

"Thank Amphitrite." was the consensus of the crowd. Then the worst thing that could have happened did. Nixi had locked eyes with Amphitrite. A wicked smile crossed the goddess's face. Amphitrite started to return to the stairs, her hand casually being dragged across the rail.

"I am not the only royalty here for this wedding," she announced. Sending another wave of excited anticipation from the crowd. Once she was back on the ship's hull, the people tried to touch her. A fact Nixi knew made Amphitrite shiver in disgust. She was not letting on that she hated the human touch. It was a price she had to pay to stroll toward Nixi.

Amphitrite was only three people away from Nixi, and Nixi was paralyzed. She did not know Amphitrite's plan but knew nothing good could happen from this appearance. Nixi tried to look away from the woman staring daggers at her.

"Let her be!" a voice called out from the stern. Nixi whipped around to see who was championing for her. Atargatis stood with her chest out as if ready to conquer anything. Amphitrite grabbed the crown of Nixi's hair pulling Nixi to her whim, and Nixi obediently followed Amphitrites' hand.

"Don't you dare hurt her!" Atargatis screamed, and to that, Amphitrite threw Nixi to the ground.

"What do I have to do to stop this?" Atargatis pleaded. She pleaded for her daughter and remained aware of all the people that could be hurt in their escalated disagreement. Atargatis looked at the door that led to the belly of the ship and nodded in its direction. Tiberus, having lived with a mute for so many months, understood immediately and started guiding people off the hull and into the belly of the ship. Amphitrite began running at full speed toward Atargatis.

"Suffer!" Amphitrite exclaimed!

"I will suffer no more!" Atargatis balled up her fist and punched the goddess. Amphitrite was surprised at the blow that hit her in the solar plexus, knocking the wind from her. Amphitrite smiled brightly.

"So we are going to fight." The thought thrilled her, and fists flew toward Atargatis. “Excellent.”

Dorus had been paralyzed when Atargatis arrived. He had seen her emerge from the water and transform into a beauty that surpassed no other. What did any of this have to do with Nixi? His brow furrowed in anger.

"I knew Nixi would make a scene," he muttered as the enchantment Amphitrite put on him created a bigger wedge of disdain for Nixi. He could have never guessed that it would lead to an immortal battle. When he finally snapped out of sheer amazement and terror, he realized he had to act. He ran to the abandoned helm and began turning the ship around. If he could get close to the banks of the coast where he lived, he may be able to get his guests to safety.

Earlier that day, his mother had told Dorus that Amphitrite, the sea goddess, would appear and bless his union. He had rolled his eyes at the thought. Goddesses tend not to take form around humans, but when he saw Amphitrite arrive, he was awestruck. He was immediately committed to marrying Jumana; the arrangement was destined to be great. A goddess had ensured it. His heart twinged in pain when he saw Nixi. He felt guilty for ending their courtship so abruptly. He had felt something he had not observed in any other relationship other than Nixi. Was it love or infatuation? The mute girl was quick to win his favor. Was she an offering from this other goddess that opposed Amphitrite? He could not trust anything. He tried to push the thoughts from his head. He needed to focus on getting to land.

Nixi was lying on the floor. She was relieved that Amphitrite had released her but feared the fight between Atargatis and Amphitrite would destroy the ship. She could not save herself or the townspeople because she could not swim. If she swallowed the button, she would gain her tail but ran the risk of getting her voice back, potentially dooming the entire boat to death.

She saw Dorus at the helm, struggling to turn the ship around. She was proud to have loved a man who would hopefully be a hero by the end of the day, saving a town single-handedly. She looked at the fist fight taking place across from Dorus. She knew she would have to try and stop it. After all, they would likely never die and be stuck in this fight forever. If she could get them off the ship, that would be a success.

Atargatis and Amphitrite might be endless, but she was not. She slipped between the two trying to push them apart, gasping in surprise when Amphitrite wrapped her arm around Nixi's throat, cutting off her air circulation. Nixi clawed at her throat. Atargatis put down her fist in defeat.

"Do whatever you want to me. I will suffer endlessly by your hands, but let her go and have an ordinary life outside your domain."

"I will do you one better. I will have your daughter suffer, and that man she loves will suffer just because Nixi looked his way." She loosened her grip, and Nixi gasped for air.

"But first," Amphitrite put her finger to her mouth as if she was thinking, and a devilish grin emerged from it.

"Let the lover see the girl for what she truly is." She threw Nixi to the ground. Nixi fell with a thud. She was once more fighting to breathe. This time by trying to hold her breath. Her legs had transformed into a tail, and she was confident she would have her voice back with her transformation.

She wanted to cry in pain, but too much was at stake. So she held herself back. If she tried, she knew she could save herself. She began to drag herself across the hull to the sea. Splinters found their way into her tail as it flickered, scraping across the floor and leaving a trail of scales.

Dorus stared at Nixi dumbfounded. It had all become clear like a curtain flung open to expose the daylight. Her ignorance that he never understood was because it was new to her. Her obsession with looking at the ocean's horizon was a longing for home. Had she done it for him? He could not process it all, haunting him for the rest of his life.

Amphitrite looked at Dorus.

"Do you like what you see?" She mocked.

"Do you love her? She wants your love so much." she teased, then followed with an exaggerated pout.

"Do you think she is worth a lifetime of suffering?" Dorus made no reply. He was instead frozen at the moment, unable to do anything. He could not answer her questions; he was overwhelmed with new, impossible information. Amphitrite started to wander toward Dorus. Nixi watched in despair. He was suffering the consequences of her actions, and she had two options. Saving herself and knowing the torment of this day, or fighting for love. She did not need to hesitate to know her answer. She looked around, searching for anything sharp. As she crawled around looking for something to help her fight, the drag of her skirt made her aware of the knife Triton had created for her birthday gift. She always kept it close as a reminder of a life she once had. She pulled the blade from the purse she had attached to her and began flopping around to attract Amphitrite's attention. When the goddess turned around, Nixi looked at her in defiance.

"He will not suffer. I will end this." She raised the intricately etched knife Triton had gifted her and plunged it into her throat. She could make no noise as she crumbled to the ground, the light of life coming to its conclusion.

Amphitrite broke out into laughter. She looked at the man taunting him.

"Oh my, oh my, oh my, I would have never seen this coming. The ignorant mermaid sacrificed herself for the likes of you." She broke out into a burst of untethered laughter.

"That's rich. So good," she sighed contently. Atargatis had run to Nixi, gathering her in her arms, and held Nixi's dead body close to her. How could she have failed her daughter so much? If she hadn't been so desperate to please her child, she would likely be happy and alive living it with all those she considered family. She saw Amphitrite making her way to the man.

"Do not touch him!" Atargatis warned.

"I care not what you do to him. He no longer matters, but killing him will halt this town's devotion to you. Is that sacrifice worth it?" Amphitrite pouted once more, making a mocking whine.

"I guess I can let it slide. Your suffering is delicious enough." A laughing Amphitrite jumped off the boat, returning to the sea again.

Atargatis brushed her daughter's face. She was caressing it softly. Dorus cautiously approached her. He felt compelled to say something, but what could mask the pain of losing a loved one? Dorus did not know who the goddess was, but he could tell that Nixi was someone she loved. So he became quiet and lightly patted her back. Then he adjusted the chairs to get the boat looking like it did before. He consoled himself that he did, in fact, love Nixi and thought about following her to his doom so that they could find each other after death. Atargatis spoke up as if she could read his thoughts.

"You should carry on with the wedding if you choose Amphotrite will keep her word about your union. There has been too much bloodshed, and Nixi would never want to have anyone pay her back with their life." She said her thoughts aloud, trying to console herself and find a reason to continue. Dorus quietly vowed always to remember her. He would carry her memory with him and live a life worthy of a debt he could never repay.

Epilogue:

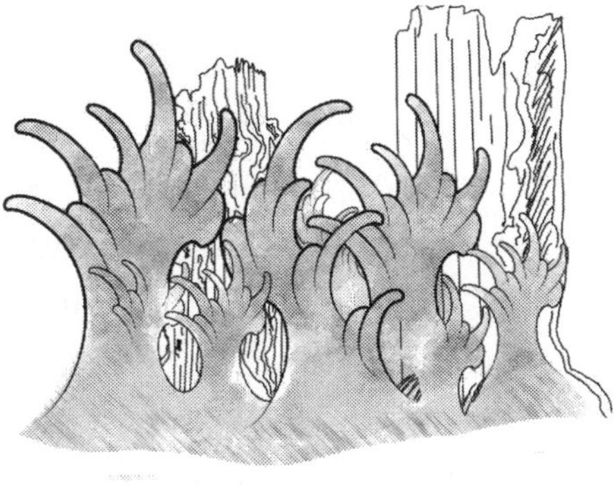

Atargatis held onto Nixi as she separated herself from the wedding by retreating to the captain's chambers. As people emerged back into the hull, she could hear them murmur about precisely what had happened. Dorus was white as a sheet perched at the helm. Amphitrite was nowhere to be found, and the goddess who opposed Amphitrite had barricaded herself in the master's quarters. The marital bed that was supposed to be for the newlyweds now was a crypt. Dorus married Jumana as planned. He did not need to love her to marry, so with great heartache, he entered into the agreement of a union. Jumana would watch her husband look longingly at the ocean for the rest of her life. He was searching for something that he would never find in her.

When the ship docked, Atargatis waited for nightfall. After the city had found its rest, she took her daughter into her arms and carried her out of the room. Both Dorus and Tiberius were waiting. Tiberius had lost his enchantment the second Nixi had died, but to replace it was a longing to have her back. He would connect closer with his family because he knew that was the only way he could honor the silent girl that appeared in their life. He offered to take the dead mermaid's body from Atargatis to give her a proper funeral, but she refused. She knew a mermaid's body was believed to provide humans with supernatural powers, and she used that knowledge to justify her not relinquishing the corpse. In truth, she just wanted to hold onto her for as long as she could, trying desperately to make up for all the years she was unable. Stricken with guilt for not fighting for her sooner.

Instead, she hid, and because of that choice, Atargatis would never be able to forgive herself. She returned to the beach, where she told Nixi about her motherhood and walked out into the sea until Nixi's body was fully submerged. The two men were eager to see if her life could be restored somehow. In a matter of minutes, the body of Nixi had turned into sea foam. The last gift that Atargatis could give her daughter. An opportunity to always be a part of where the ocean meets the sea.

The men both fell to their knees as the foam washed ashore. They cried, and when Atargatis returned to the banks, they begged to also be marked with Nixi's essence. She placed a handful of sea foam in each of their mouths. Atargatis instructed them to swallow it.

"Now," Atargatis said in a low somber tone,

"When a human dies, you'll have a chance to find her. If you do, then your corpse shall bubble at the mouth." The men bowed to Atargatis, shedding the tears that Atargatis was too numb to manifest herself before returning to their lives. She walked along the banks of the sea. Occasionally the sea foam would lap at her feet, and she would smile. She had always wanted to connect with her child.

One night, as Atargatis walked on the edge of two worlds, she came upon a cliff. At the bottom of the cliff, an abundant collection of seafoam swirled around caught between the rocks. Atargatis swam to the spot. She had finally found the tears that had eluded her. She did not move from this collection of her child and became a stone soaked in the remnants of her daughter. The whistle of her sobs still haunts the spot as if the wind was reaching out, reminding the world of her tears. Amphitrite, still watching her nemesis, had seen Atargatis turn into a stone and once more resumed her quest to see Atargatis suffer. Amphitrite now sends waves to lash at that stone, slowly eroding Atargatis with time.

Made in the USA
Columbia, SC
27 April 2024

34950297R00109